THE
GAMBLERS
PARADOX

THE
GAMBLERS
PARADOX

P.N. "Harry" Harish

PARTRIDGE
A Penguin Random House Company

p_n_harish@hotmail.com

To order additional copies of this book, contact
Partridge India
000 800 10062 62
www.partridgepublishing.com/india
orders.india@partridgepublishing.com

CONTENTS

Chapter 1:   The Murder and the Maid 1

Chapter 2:   The Whiff of Money 23

Chapter 3:   The Relaxed Banter and the Epiphany 36

Chapter 4:   The Search and the Ladder 40

Chapter 5:   The Secrets of the Money 54

Chapter 6:   The Open and Shut Case 63

Chapter 7:   Follow the Money! 76

Chapter 8:   It's a Numbers Game 81

Chapter 9:   The Links of a Chain 88

Chapter 10: The Quest for the Connection 105

Chapter 11: The Player in the Game 114

Chapter 12: The Heat is On! 128

Chapter 13: Back to School 145

Chapter 14: The Certainties: Death and Taxes 166

Chapter 15: A Call from the Grave 191

Chapter 16: Gambling Pays 202

For Abhishek & Nikita with Love

Chapter 1

THE MURDER AND THE MAID

The radio came on loud and clear, the Dispatcher spoke slowly and clearly as though speaking to a child. "Report of a dead male in Easton Villa place", she then gave the address and asked patrol cars nearby to response. Taggart and his partner Devlin in the patrol car quickly put away the donuts they had been eating. Taggart turned the car around and headed North West to come on to the highway. Siren blaring and tires squealing they sped to the scene. San Carlos at this hour on a Sunday morning was quiet and traffic light. Taggart was the relative veteran in the team. Driving without much anxiety he was the opposite of Devlin, who was excited and it showed in the way that he kept his eyes on the radio on the dashboard. The Dispatcher came on once again, "Possible Homicide, officers respond with caution". This only increased Devlin's excitement. Would he have to approach the scene with gun drawn? Would he have to put his hands in front and tell people on the sidewalk to move away from the scene?

Taggart felt no such thrill in fact he was blasé about the call, yeah! Someone had copped it. He knew where Easton Villa was, a quiet place, mostly single family homes and there would be no one on the street not on a Sunday and not this early in the day.

As they sped along, more info on the radio, the dead had been tentatively identified as Prof. Dennis McPherson, aged 56 intoned the speaker, living in Easton Villa since 1980, Taggart wondered which data base the detectives desk had looked into, these days everything was in some data base and the police had access to them all, Taggart mused that the police knew you better than your own mother. All the known facts on the victim within 5 minutes of the first report.

Taggart made a sharp left onto the road that would lead to Easton Villa and a mile down the road turned into Easton Villa, as he expected there was no one on the road, no cars, just a quiet street. The road lay straight with houses generously spread on half acre lots. As he drove down he could spot a woman waving at the approaching patrol car. She was standing at the end of a short driveway and he could not turn the cruiser to the driveway, pulling up along the sidewalk, both patrolmen jumped out and drew their guns. Devlin quicker on the draw as if he had been practicing this move, Taggart more measured. In the squad they were known as the T&D team, short for Tackle and Dodge, the tactics they had displayed in an impromptu match at the retirement party for the last Chief.

Taggart looked around, could not spot any activity in the houses around, he looked up at the house, the front door was wide open, the woman was babbling now, the Prof was dead, shot in the face is what they gathered. Taggart gathered that she was the help who came in twice a week to clean and keep house. They went into the house, the maid pointed up the stairs and they quickly went up, their steps loud in the quiet house.

They entered the first door on the right, a wide door and the scene of the crime. The professor was in his chair sitting facing a desk, his head thrown back, and a dark hole in the forehead. Taggart holstered his gun and bent over the victim. The eyes were open and lifeless. A small drop of blood in the corner of one eye. Taggart bent down to look at the back of the head, no exit wound. So the killer had used a hollow point, at least that's what Taggart recalled from his firearms training. That also explained the blood in the corner of the eye, isn't that what a hollow point did, mash everything in the skull?

"The victim has been shot gangland style" he told Devlin.

"You think he has been killed by a gang?" asked Devlin.

"I said gangland style, hollow point bullet!!" explained Taggart feeling superior to the rookie on his team.

"So gang members buy these bullets and hollow them to make the target a sure kill? Devlin asked.

Taggart shook his head, "You don't buy a bullet and hollow them, they come that way, everyone uses hollow point, I use and I suppose you do too."

"No, I don't, I use department issue" Devlin quite horrified being told that he would deliberately use hollow point bullet to make a sure kill.

"What do you think the department gives you?" Taggart said turning away to see the rest of the scene. It was the professor's study, the walls were lined with shelves, and all the walls including the space above the door, Taggart looked up to see that the attic had been opened up and the shelves reached the very top of the house. In the corner he saw a collapsing ladder which could be pushed up against the wall or pulled down to reach the higher shelves.

He turned and saw Devlin leaning over the edge of the professor's desk to look out the window.

"Hey, hey, get back from that window before you contaminate the crime scene" he shouted.

Devlin quickly stepped back saying "I didn't touch anything! This window is open and the shooter could have shot him from outside". Yes, the window was open, the pane pushed aside along the wall, a sliding window.

Taggart thought that odd, he had a vague impression that this was a Spanish style house; did these old homes come with sliding windows? Probably the professor had re done the house to suit him. The desk was flush with the window, was it to allow light as the professor sat at the desk to read?

Hearing sirens approaching the house they hurried out of the study and came down to the driveway, Devlin hurried to their car and fetched the Crime scene tape and started to string them around the trees in the front yard. Taggart spoke to the distraught maid "ELLE", who was more composed now, but her distress was obvious. Taggart noted that she was quite good looking, dressed chic! A white blouse and pleated skirt, making her out to be more an office going working woman than a part time maid.

The cruisers that had pulled up were from Redwood City police, out of their jurisdiction by a few streets, pulled to the scene of a crime by curiosity and by now the incessant chatter on the police waves. Taggart waved at them and went to the sidewalk to an unmarked vehicle that had just pulled up. Out stepped Detective Gregg Harvey, tall and lean, long and lanky hair turned grey prematurely. He couldn't be a day older than Taggart but seemed more world weary and wary of his surroundings.

"So?" he asked Taggart laconically. Taggart told him the only thing that he had gathered so far "Somebody shot the victim through an open window" he said turning and pointing at the window on the upper floor on the right of the main door.

Det. Gregg pointed at the maid Elle and "Who is that?" "That's the housekeeping woman who called it in".

"Did you check out the house?" Another rapid fire question from Det. Gregg.

Taggart shook his head, "We came in and she pointed us upstairs and we went into the study saw the victim in his chair and he is very dead, he has a hole in his head".

"Yeah, shot through that window there, no bullet casings in the room, I checked" added Devlin helpfully.

Gregg Harvey turned his full attention to Devlin, "Anything else?"

Devlin shook his head "he has a whole lot of books in there".

"So?" Gregg Harvey questioned the rookie.

"Well, he is a professor you know" Devlin finished lamely.

Det. Gregg hadn't finished with him, "Did you ask that woman's permission to enter the house?"

"No, but she was the one who called 911" Devlin pointed out.

"How do you know?"

"We'll have the recording of that call, she can't deny that"

"How would you know if the judge would permit the log of calls to be admitted as evidence?"

"But, why would she deny making the call" Devlin couldn't believe any one calling in a murder would be unreasonable to deny it later in court.

Det. Gregg Harvey shook his head at this level of understanding of the criminal justice system in the country. "Suppose we go in there now and we find evidence that directly links her with the crime, that evidence may be inadmissible in court, as a product of illegal search & seizure".

"A Judge would do that?" asked the incredulous Devlin "you can't be serious!"

"Am I not being serious now?" flat tones but no mistaking the rhetoric.

"What's a responding officer to do, the dispatcher puts out the call, we rush, find the 911 caller—who points, we find the body and the perpetrator walks?"

Harvey decided to lay it down for them in clear terms "You come on the location, ASK her "Did you make a 911 call?", "Did you say someone was shot?", "Do you live here?", "Do you work here?", "Can we enter the house?" and she says OK, you then enter the house and if then you find she has shot her employer, you cuff her!!", It's called probable cause!".

"Probable cause? Yeah we have a 911 call". Devlin was now pleading.

"You have probable cause to believe someone has been shot, but no probable cause to ENTER that house, if someone is present who can permit or deny you that permission".

Taggart was aware of some of this, specially the entry to a house, except, on a call of domestic violence called in by the battered wife or a neighbor, then the officer could enter, try and break up the fight, too bad if the responding officer got shot. If he was lucky enough not to get shot then he could cuff the violent villain and haul him off to the lock up. Usually the wife refused to press charges and the by now sober villain walked off arm in arm with his mate. No booking him on drunk & disorderly either, for that you had to take him to a hospital to draw blood. Taggart recalled wryly the case where an entire team at a station received training on drawing blood so that they could avoid a trip to the hospital, the accused challenged this procedure, the prosecutor brought in the doctor who had offered the training, no question that the Doctor knew his job, yes the training is the same as he would give a medical technician, but the final question was WHO approved the training? Did any authority in Medical Education approve this training? NO? Out went the blood test. Ah! The thickets of law!

Meanwhile, Det. Gregg Harvey approached Elle and asked her permission to enter the house; she appeared surprised at the request, but nodded. Harvey repeated the question, Elle who—exasperated, whispered—Yes.

They then entered the house, Devlin pointed up the stairs, but ignoring him Harvey continued on the ground floor, noted the basement door was open, peeped in and seemed to lose interest. "No windows, door is closed" he explained to Taggart following him behind. Same in the kitchen, he looked around opened the door to the backyard. The backyard appeared as big as the front, or even bigger, it had a lap pool, high fencing all around, a fireplace and an outdoor kitchen. He wondered, when did people living here ever use the backyard outdoor fireplace or kitchen; he knew that the victim was known to be living alone.

Re-entering the kitchen they made their way upstairs, there Harvey barely looked at the Victim and turned his attention to the books on the shelves all around. At first it appeared to him that they had been arranged haphazardly, Not a regular library system, no Dewey decimal system here. Then he noted a pattern. The majority of the books were Mathematics and Statistics. The mathematics was arranged subject wise, alphabetically. So there were big sections of books on a single subject, he noted in passing that Probability was a big section. He moved on to Statistics and noted the same, in this too Probability seemed to have a big section, and he wondered what set the subject apart in the two disciplines.

The rest of the house was unremarkable; it was big, sure, but no disorder and not even a sense of being disturbed by the daily life in a house. Harvey paused in the Main bedroom and saw the bed neatly done, so maybe Professor had not slept in it last night. So was he shot last night as he was in his study? If it was late why was the window open? So many questions, the answers would take some time to dig up.

He then led them both downstairs saying "Let Forensics finish first". When they were in the front Harvey turned abruptly to Taggart and said "You are on my team for the investigation, I spoke to the chief and he approves".

Taggart avoided looking at Devlin, would he leave his partner and join the elite in the Homicide Squad? And much to Taggart's relief, Harvey then added "You both are my main diggers, sniffers, hunters and I want to not feel sorry for myself for landing such a case. This, mark my words, is a difficult case".

"Difficult?" the T&D team chorused.

"Yes, difficult, see in a Homicide, you need a villain who can kill, a dark figure you imagine that could have done the deed, he or she should be thought of as a killer, if you feel that you can focus on such figure you can zero in on some suspects, here it is not possible, who would want to kill a university teacher in his own study as he is peacefully reading his beloved books."

He went on more thoughtfully "It's probably not the wife, would she have to climb a ladder to his study to shoot him?" see that scratch mark where the ladder rested against the window sill?"

They both looked up at the window and the scratch marks, chastened that they had missed it.

"Look at our victim" continued Harvey "A professor who lives quietly, look at this house, he's been living here since 1980, and he bought it for what? A hundred grand? Two? And what's it today in these parts two million? Look at that Car" he pointed at the cars in the driveway.

Taggart noted one Volvo and a Porsche, Harvey obviously meant for them to look at the Porsche, so even Harvey was capable of making assumptions. Looking at Elle standing quietly with a sad face, he could imagine that such a woman catching the eye of a rich guy, the rich, may be married, guy buys her a Porsche, it's possible. Yet Harvey could be right and the victim had fancy wheels.

Harvey continued in the assessment of the case, "It costs a packet, not exactly the kind you would expect a college Don to be driving around, though I don't know what the Universities pay nowadays, a house with six bedrooms, a flashy car, a backyard pool, the guy lived well, not super rich to draw attention to himself, but better than most, and one thing that I did notice and think strange is that there is no safe in the house, not in the study, nor in the bedrooms, not on the walls, all the walls seem the same thickness, anyway Forensics will tell us of any safes, so where does he keep the valuables, his papers?".

Devlin having regained his poise interjected "Maybe in the desk, that's a huge contraption, the prof had pushed his chair all the way in, that's why I think the chair didn't topple when he was shot".

Harvey thought maybe Devlin wasn't such a loss after all. About to say something, Harvey spotted Tilden emerge from the front door and reached him with long strides. Bill Tilden carried the title of Supervisor of Forensics, but he was a field man and the spot man for every kind of crime in the large area down from San Mateo to well down south in the peninsula. He had to be handled delicately, very touchy since the last few years after a botched fingerprint test. As it happened, Tilden gave testimony on the identification of the accused based on a faxed print, on the stand he reiterated that "Believe me I know what I am doing", this proved his undoing, the match was wrong and a report on the wrong conclusion circulated nationwide. Damaging his reputation and embittered him, now he followed his own axiom of repeating the process for every test, even blood tests for DUI's, there was a huge backlog in the lab, but the lab was the only one accredited for Forensics in the vast area.

San Carlos had no lab, no crime, and no budget and quietly paid its share for the services of the Lab at Redwood City, Murder was even more of a rarity; last one was 6 years ago. City Police chiefs generally kept the Homicide detectives in their good books, you never knew when you would need them in your own backyard.

Harvey came up on Tilden and asked him "Hi! Bill, what can you tell me?" fully expecting Tilden to say the report will be with you soon.

But Tilden paused, hesitating to come up with what he had found, but with a puzzled look told Harvey "You know the house is clean of prints, no latents, nothing at all in the lower floor, some in the upper, all of it the victims, it's quite unlike a house where a man has been living, wiped clean!".

Harvey's gaze shifted uneasily towards the maid Elle who stood still with a fixed stare, Tilden noted her and said, "We will need her prints, and by the way, the guy from the coroners' office is also here, the victim died of gunshot wound to the head another thing is that it looks as If someone squeezed his throat, but he was already dead, mind you, It was not strangulation his hyoid bone is not broken, but somebody held him by the throat after he died!".

Harvey looked at the forensic man in surprise, he was sure there were no signs of forced entry not in the front or back, the basement was tiny and the door shut inward, anyone kicking in that door from the outside would have a fractured leg, so who entered the house?, surely the killer didn't go up a ladder, shoot the victim, climb down and enter the house and try and squeeze whatever life was left in the Professor. If the shooter had gone in through the window there surely would have been some signs on the desk.

The question "You Sure?" didn't pass Harvey's lips. He knew that it was certain to alienate him from Tilden. Sure! had been Tilden's response on that witness stand and he had regretted it ever since. He regretted more that he had relied on the Fax print for identification rather than the actual from the scene. That botched identification forever damaging him; he who had laid out the science of collecting evidence was passed over and remained a supervisor while newbies with degrees in arts were becoming Directors of Crime Labs. So Harvey became sure that Tilden was sure.

Thoroughly dispirited at the growing number of unknowns in this case, that too in a space of half hour, he asked Tilden, "Anything in the desk?"

"Oh, Yes, there's all sorts of papers in there, bills, notes, books, you know he has used notebooks like a diary, not like a record of his daily life more like notes on the day's work, all noted with time and date. That desk is big, one time I think there were drawers that could be opened from both sides of the desk, it has been modified and so you can pull one drawer and at the back there is one more drawer that you can pull out, some really old papers are there, the document man is now bagging it now very carefully preserving every fold in every sheet as if they have some clues, anyway it will take all day, tomorrow come by the lab and you can dig in yourself".

With that Tilden went off towards the big white "Crime Lab on Wheels" Van, it was virtually his home. That van was the pride of the county, available 24X7 and fully equipped to deal with all that was necessary for solving crime. Not many counties in California could boast of such an asset, it set them apart and showed that they were in the forefront of technology. Law enforcement claimed that conviction rate in California was better than the national average because of their progress in technology. The fact that repeat offenders aided this bit of statistic was ignored. Once convicted everything about the felon was on record, so it was easy, a break in and a safe cracked?, the detective crew just asked, "Hey, give a list of all those who have disabled security alarm, add those who have cracked a safe, and please give the names of those who are on parole" and voila the bugger was back in prison. Rather than reform parole regulations, the state law makers passed the "Three Strikes Law", like it's a game, three strikes and you are OUT, Baseball is as American as it can get. The theory was good, give a convicted felon an incentive not to go his old ways, retrain and find a job, not a hold up job! The incentive? Not having to spend the rest of life in prison with the Judge tagging on the sentence of the earlier convictions to the latest and sending him away.

Anyway, now Felons out on parole, particularly those who were one strike shy of three, regularly shot their victims or witnesses. Murder will happen, hey California is the largest state and biggest in terms of migrants the unhealthy mix of misfits, what you expect?

Harvey turned his attention back to the investigation; he walked up to Elle and to strike a rapport, asked her genially, "So, how long have you been in America?" Wrong question, here in California that meant you were asking if they were illegal immigrant. Elle bridled at the question, "I am a naturalized citizen".

Harvey was sorry, she didn't know how sorry he was, but he was sorry at his attempt at making a connection should start off with his subject drawing the wrong implication. He started once again, "Where are you from, I mean which country?" "Honduras" she replied. He would have never guessed. For one she was certainly

Hispanic which meant a lot of ethnic groups, but she was fairer than from people down south who always seemed to have a tan.

Honduras meant little to him except that it was the nearest Exotic destination from California; he suddenly recalled uneasily that Honduras was where the highest murder rate in the world was. During the sensitivity briefing the department gave its officers, the instructor remarked that in Honduras 1 in a 1000 citizen was likely to be offed by his fellow citizen within the year, at that same rate in the United States, the instructor concluded, there would be a quarter million homicides.

Is it possible that this pretty woman came up from Honduras with murder in her Genes? Harvey dismissed the thought.

"I need to ask a few questions now and later you have to come in and give a statement at the precinct that OK with you?"

"Yes" curt, she was still miffed.

He switched to a formal tone for his next question, "How long have you worked for Prof, McPherson?"

"Eight years" and then she added "Ever since I got to U.S.".

So, a loyal servant, bound to know her employer well, "Is that so? How come?"

"Well, he was with a volunteer group that worked on Honduras after Mitch and he spotted me and got me help back there, but three years later he came and helped me get here with my two children"

"Mitch, what?" Harvey was puzzled. She seemed surprised by the question, surely everyone had heard of Mitch, the big storm. She explained how she had to leave her village, when her parents were killed in that storm.

Wisely stopping himself from asking about the father of the children, Harvey ploughed on, "He helped you did he? So you got along well with him?"

This seemed to him a better line of questioning than asking, what was your relationship with the dead guy? She might think that he was suggesting that there might be more to the connection between the victim and her.

"Oh, He was the sweetest man I ever met, the best man I have ever met" she didn't gush or give the impression of a star struck employee but as someone who simply loved the dead guy. With that Harvey ruled her out as a possible candidate for the dark figure that he had told his team about.

He turned the questions to the professor himself, "What happened to his wife and Kids?"

"Nothing happened to the wife and kids, they are in India!"

"Oh, I am sorry, I assumed that he was single and divorced and I have seen the photos on the wall in the family room and you know it happens, the guy living alone, no one else in the house, so what happened that his family simply moved away to India?".

"Miriam, that's the wife, was always interested in music, especially in Indian music, she wanted to study the Veena, you know the very big guitar like thing, that's too big to carry around so that you sit on the ground and play, she wanted to go to Mysore which is a town in India to learn that, the son followed her a year later".

With that Harvey felt that he had added to his knowledge of musical instruments, but not much in the way of the victim's family life.

"So what else can you tell me about Miriam, you said that you have been here 8 years."

"She was, is a sweet lady, completely supported her husband in everything he did, but without sounding disloyal in any way, I have to say, she was exactly like me, completely devoted to him, she was his willing slave".

"So, why did the son go to India, he isn't in college? How old is he?"

"he's twenty two now, he was studying art at Stanford and then decided to join a project for preserving some cave paintings somewhere near Mumbai in India, the university is sponsoring the team, I am sorry if I gave the impression that he went down to India only to be with his mother, she is in a city called Mysore, they are not together but meet over weekends".

A little defensive and also not very forthcoming about the son, Harvey wondered why she was being very clinical speaking about the son, as though keeping any emotion out was very important.

Harvey asked her if she knew how to contact the wife and son saying "I need to call them and give the sad news".

"Oh! I have already called, both are coming in on the same flight, they should be here by Monday night".

This was another surprise for Harvey, in all the time that he had watched her he hadn't noticed her reaching for a phone. He had missed that and had to wonder when she had actually called them.

"Must have been difficult making that call, you being with the family for so long" nudging her for some details on the relationships in the house.

Elle looked puzzled as she said, "Yes, the most horrible thing I had to do in my life after coming to America, Miriam was distraught, she kept saying I told him it was dangerous but he ignored me, I asked her what danger and from whom?, but she said you wouldn't understand. I have no idea what she was talking about".

For a brief moment Harvey felt elated, here is the first glimmer that someone knows what led to this murder, where all was dark, some light, his assessment that this might be an unsolved case changed. Mentally berating himself for his selfish motives and keeping the anxiety out of his voice asked her "You sure they will be here Monday?"

"Yes, they should be here, they are coming in by way of Hong Kong".

Harvey finally came to the question that he should have asked first, "What happened when you came in this morning?"

She began "On Sundays I start early from home by 6.30 and . . ." Harvey interrupted her "where's your house?"

"Over in Friendly Acres, you know the place?" Harvey nodded and Elle continued "and in the holiday traffic it takes me about 10 minutes to get here, I came and went in and did the ground floor, the kitchen and then went up and made the bed and then went into the study and I saw him, usually when I don't see him in the living room I assume that he is in the study and don't call out".

That explained the no prints and wiped clean report from Bill Tilden. No mystery there, the maid did it not a butler, one unknown vanished. Harvey's mood got better.

Harvey asked her about the kitchen, Elle said, "It was usual, some plates were in the sink and I put them in the dishwasher".

The crime scene people would have collected the empty food packs that will clear up one detail.

Something else struck him, "Is there or was there a ladder in the house?"

"No, what ladder?" asked Elle.

"You know the ladder to climb up and may be clean the windows, a long one".

"No ladders!" Elle was positive, then with a slight smile she said "Den was not a handyman around the house, he always called in someone to do the pool, trim the hedges and the trees".

Harvey's puzzle of the ladder continued, who brought in a ladder, who removed a ladder? Where did the ladder go?

"No wonder the house looks neat and fresh" he said to her.

"Yes, it also got a coat of fresh paint this week" Elle added. Harvey hadn't smelt fresh paint, but pushed the thought aside, what's paint got to do with murder.

With that he bid good bye to her and said that he would call about a formal statement at the precinct sometime in the coming week. She said that he would have to let her know in advance for her to get time off from work. "Sure, what agency do you work for?" he asked and got the most unexpected answer.

"I don't work for any agency; I work for Trigent Research as the Spanish interface with our South American clients".

Harvey gaped, all the more, since his first impression of her that she was well dressed and had a poise which he had ignored but stereotyped as a maid.

She saw his confusion and explained "Den was particular that I get some education and skills and he made sure that I qualified in Linguistics and software and then he got me working at Trigent, where he is, was, a Director" Having corrected herself she became pensive and having exchanged contact numbers with her, he led her to the car.

Chapter 2

THE WHIFF OF MONEY

He stood at the kerb and watched as she drove away, Harvey noted that with the house facing northwest the morning sun was coming up behind the house, the trees in front of the house cast long diagonal shadows across the road. A few residents had come out of their houses and stood outside the police tape, they were a subdued lot. Harvey would have to ask that Taggart & Devlin to canvas the neighbors to find If they had noticed anything. It would be routine and probably a waste of time but had to be done by the book.

Taggart and Devlin walked up to their new boss and asked him if it was alright to allow her to drive the car away, shouldn't the tech guys have a look first?

"No, it's alright, I think it's safe to say that at this point she is not suspect" replied Harvey.

Taggart & Devlin exchanged looks. Devlin spoke up, "Everything all right? She was giving you tough looks!?"

"It's OK, we got off on the wrong foot, she's cleared up some minor things, and she's the one who wiped the fingerprints. Also there was no ladder in the house; it seems that Prof was not a general handyman around the house. That's got me wondering about the ladder. Can you guys think of anything about that?

They both shook their heads. The image of a murderer carrying away a ladder was a bit much to imagine.

Harvey said "Let's check the perimeter once again", saying that he started around the right side of the house, the windows on this side were the sealed type, again a new feature that old style Spanish houses wouldn't have had.

They rounded the house and came up to the lap pool, looking in, it was clear that the pool had been cleaned recently, there were no leaves or other debris floating, the pool floor also looked clean. They would have to check the pool maintenance man's schedule. The tennis court on the right of the pool was also well maintained. The whole property was like a show piece that was being listed for sale. That gave Harvey an idea and he turned to Taggart and asked him to check with local real estate agencies if the property had been listed.

If it was listed then it would point to the professors plan to move away, was he sensing danger? But there were no security measures around the house, no motion sensors, no CCTV Cameras, not even yard lighting, except the lights for the Tennis Court.

What Elle had told him of her talk with Miriam the Professors wife, was playing on his mind. What danger was she talking about? Harvey could not wait for Monday and the interview with her.

The door to the basement was set at a lower level in the backyard, a couple of steps led down to it, Harvey tried the door pulling it towards him and it swung open easily. He had noted that the door had been latched when he checked it earlier, so the forensics team must have covered this part of the house and moved away which explained the door being open. The basement was really small, the electrical and the heating were all on one end of it, the rest of the floor was a jumble of stuff, discarded furniture, mattresses. This was the only part of the house that was disorganized. A number of Tennis rackets were hung on the wall, so there were regular players in the house.

There was nothing in that place that seemed to have any connection to the murder upstairs, but Harvey had an uneasy feeling. He refused to call these feelings as a hunch, he got them often, he called it "Clairvoyance", his wife Susan made fun of him about it, sometimes too derisively for his comfort.

They went up to the main floor and looked in all the rooms once again, spotting nothing unusual or out of place. They reached the Study where the document man was still busy digging out the papers from the huge desk. Harvey made a mental note to go over to the Lab and look through the papers.

There was a humming noise in the room and Harvey looked up at the ceiling, with the Attic floor removed to extend the study upward to put up the shelves, the vent fan under the roof was working and filled the room with a steady hum. The fan pulled the air in the house and vented it out through the roof filling the house with fresh air and cooling it in the summer. Harvey then remembered Elle telling him that the house had got a new coat of paint during the week; maybe the fan cleared the smell. He turned to Taggart and asked, "Did you smell fresh paint in the house?"

Taggart said no he hadn't smelt new paint. But looking around, admitted everything looked fresh and neat and could have received a painting. They had to follow up on that as well.

The body had been removed and now maybe on its way to the Medical Examiner's office for the autopsy. Harvey approached the desk and noted that it was at least four feet wide and he realized that even bending across the desk one could not reach the window. The document man watching him helpfully pointed at a button on the desk that activated the window to open and close. That meant that the Professor had opened the window, was it open before the killer came up on the ladder or did someone known to him come up and asked him to open?. It was more likely that the killer noticing the open window came up on the ladder and shot him. Then again there was the unexplained attempt to choke the victim after he was shot, the killer was in this study and vanished without a trace. Elle had wiped the place downstairs but not here, but here too there were no prints found.

Harvey turned his attention to the document man and asked "Anything in here interesting?"

The document man brightened "There are a lot of bank statements; It seems the Vic had bank accounts all over the place, Lots of money in those banks!" Harvey wasn't too surprised after all the guy was a Don at the university and got paid well and maybe he got grants too, whenever Harvey read in the Newspapers that the Federal Government is sponsoring research into this and that and the amounts mentioned, he had wondered where all the money went. It seems that the Federal money went to people like Prof. Dennis McPherson.

"He paid lots of Taxes too!" There was awe in the Document Man's voice.

"How much?" Harvey was unprepared for the answer.

"A hundred thousand last year in State Tax!"

A stunned Harvey did some quick mental calculation and exclaimed, "That's about one million in the year?" He could not reconcile that fact with what he believed a University teacher earned. To be sure they earned better than most, maybe a lot better than a lot of other people.

He looked around and told himself, this is a median income house, median income being the income that people around you earned. He was sure that if he could put together the Tax returns of all the people in this part of San Carlos the income of each would be similar, give or take a few dollars. Harvey could have held forth on his radical view that Median Income brought out the egalitarianism that other systems just couldn't get close, Reach the Median Income and have the status, less than that you don't count, more and you are the chosen few of the gods.

People with less than median income did not live in single family homes with lap pools. People with Median income lived in houses like this with lap pools and tennis court and paid mortgage for the next 30 years.

With the kind of Taxes that Prof. Den McPherson paid, his house should have been in a gated community with private security manning the gates 24X7. McPherson was about a hundred leagues ahead of the median income people.

What was McPherson, an ascetic, austere patriarch, simple living and high thinking while the money piled up in the banks? Even the Porsche that he seemed to prefer didn't count, you would expect Rolls Royce's, Bentleys or some such, and of course Chauffer driven.

Who were the people who knew that he had this kind of money?, His accountant who prepared the Tax Returns for sure or may be his Wealth Advisers, an army of whom had set up offices in Redwood Shores development sharing that exclusive enclave with billion dollar tech companies. His family? All of who could be considered Potential Suspects.

Tomorrow he would have a few answers to this question and who knows maybe pick up a few tips on making that kind of money himself, Susan would be pleased, she wanted to get out of the Median Income bracket and do volunteer social work and get the awards that they seem to give away to such large hearted people. Susan's last foray into volunteer prominence did not end well, the revival church was promoted by a charismatic pastor, who strutted across the stage three times on the holy Sabbath, introduced foot stomping music, let out Hallelujah's to shake the stained glass windows and who mentioned his devoted wife at least once during the sermon, to say how much a family man he was, who spoke of taking the Caltrain to distant suburbs to be with a family of a very sick child, the common touch that, taking the train and not his limousine. The IRS, less forgiving than the Bible says you ought to be, busted him for Tax Evasion and the judge then sent him away to study the inscrutable ways of the Lord in the confines of a cell. There were rumors that he had in prison demanded that he be allowed to hold service and deliver the sermons, which the warden after some hesitation allowed. But his trial and downfall was still receiving extensive TV coverage and the inmates ever wise in the ways of the world demanded protection money and he hastily withdrew serving mankind for the while. The upshot of which was Susan distanced herself from the church with alacrity.

Harvey shook off the reverie that he had fallen into, finding the money had done that, no not finding the money, the whiff of money had done that, and then inexorably the thoughts had turned to that of his wife. Determined to keep his focus on the job he looked around to find that Taggart and Devlin were missing.

In the foyer he found Devlin intently staring at a photo on the wall. Devlin turned to Harvey with the look of someone who had found some secret.

"You know Chief, I almost did not recognize the house in this photograph, yes it is this house all right covered up with creepers, you can't see anything but the doors and the windows, the creepers cover all the walls on the outside".

Harvey leaned in to look and saw that indeed the house was unrecognizable as this house. He immediately thought of Elle to find some answers. He pulled out his cell phone and punched up the numbers he had taken just a while ago. While waiting for her to pick up the phone he thought, maybe I am just eager to talk to her about anything, not just some old creepers.

Then the voice on the other end "Yes" in a dull voice, Harvey sensed her grief, while she had maintained her poise right through the morning, in the privacy of her home she was probably grieving for the one person who, he surmised, was both her savior and mentor and she the protégé.

"Harvey here, say can you tell me when the creepers in the front were cut down?" He could not have told her why that was important in the investigation. He just needed to know and from her right at this moment, if only on the phone. The heart and mind are both unreasonable . . . at times.

"Just last week" her tone did not imply that the question was in any way irrelevant. Then, in a matter fact way, she launched into the explanation "they were very old, the branches thick as tree trunks and they were slowly damaging the house, at the top they had reached the attic roof and it was getting warped, plus the inside walls were getting damp damage, only the study with its hardwood paneling was spared. In fact all the dry walls in the front were replaced and then the paint job".

For Harvey and his team this opened another line for enquiry, who cut down the creeper, who painted the house, who supervised the work and could any of them have a hand in the death of a harmless university don.

"Who did the work?"

"Someone named Lee brothers they were the only ones who would do the removal and the paint job, they came down from Burlingame up north on Bayshore highway, and you can find them in the book"

So forthcoming was she on this enquiry that Harvey decided to seek more on the house, he had asked Taggart to find if the house had been listed with a local real estate for sale, now he could chance it with Elle, maybe she knew.

"Elle, can you tell me if the house is listed for sale?"

"Sure it has been on the market for 2 weeks now, actually it's the Agent who suggested that the creeper be removed and the house spruced up to fetch a better price, Elizabeth Ann that's the agent, she said that the house would fetch more and that if it had come on the market say two years ago it would have gone for 3, you know, million, now she said to expect offers closer to 2".

To Harvey this information meant that the Victim had decided to move away but WHY? Did he sense danger or receive a threat?

"Where was he moving to?"

"To Napa Valley, you know the Wine Country?" Harvey felt a slight, of course he knew Napa Valley, tourists were pouring into it to taste California wine and giving the French a run for their money, why did she think that he wouldn't know something in his own state?.

Elle oblivious to his reaction went on "Dennis has bought a big place and he was there last week when the house was a mess because of the work going on". No sooner had she finished speaking quite genially, he shot her a question, police style, and "Do you know how much that place cost?" the money bug having truly bitten him.

"Hey, How the hell would I know how much it cost, I didn't buy that place, Dennis did" Elle responded spiritedly.

A frisson of excitement went through Harvey, she was saying—Hey and Hell to him, was she feeling that familiar with him?

He thanked her in his best conciliatory voice and hung up.

Outside the house, Harvey decided that it was time to wind up at the scene of the crime. He gathered his team and asked them if they thought if they needed to do anything else. Taggart & Devlin on their feet for a good six hours now, surviving on the breakfast of frosted donuts that was so frustratingly interrupted, had to deny that they had any fresh initiative.

Taggart said "We need to know more about the professor at his work place, the Univ".

Devlin was quick to pounce, "It's Sunday, in the afternoon, you will get zilch in that place, all the great big buildings will be locked down, the faculty won't answer any doorbells, and the students will be trying to recover from the week end of excess for tomorrows grind". All said in a single breath.

Harvey and Taggart looked at each other and laughed, the first time in the day that they felt that way. They quickly stopped themselves. Levity and Murder does not go too well together. In this century it was the all-pervasive media cameras and surveillance cameras. A media camera may catch them or the CC TV of the neighbor might, either way they would be the photo feature in the media.

COPS WERE SEEN LAUGHING AT THE SCENE OF THE GHASTLY GANGLAND KILLING OF WELL LOVED PROFESSOR.

Sample captions for news starved networks.

Harvey agreed, "Yeah, let's go someplace and sit down and get together what we have till now, this place is beginning to get on my nerves, let's check if the crime scene people are ready to leave".

As if on cue the Forensics team came out the door and joined them, one of them handed Harvey a leather pouch which was heavy saying "Those are some keys we found in the study, they are tagged for some bank lockers, you might want to look at them and we also found the personal computer of the victim, it was under all those books on the desk, it had live streaming video from some casino tables, I suppose Tilden will tell you about it".

Devlin the fast maturing student of criminal investigation asked him, "Do you have to get a court order to open those lockers?"

Harvey began to expound "Nah, in a murder case, the property and person of a dead man is fair game", and then he bit his tongue.

Increasingly there had been reports, that confiscated property had been missing from the evidence lockers and search & seizure raids also yielded less stuff than subsequently claimed by the felons themselves, the policemen were helping themselves!.

Hastily correcting himself, Harvey said, "What I mean to say is that in murder cases, in the absence of next-of-kin, the investigators can probe all properties and possessions of the deceased without having to obtain a formal order of the court, it's not against the provisions of the constitution, it's not invasion of privacy".

Devlin looked at Harvey with undisguised admiration, that's the way he wanted to talk to people, expounding constitutional principles and upholding the power and dignity of law enforcement.

Harvey asked them to suggest a place where they could catch up and analyze the day's events and to pursue, which of there were now numerous lines, the investigation tomorrow.

They decided to go to a place on El Camino real that Devlin said is the best, Taggart agreed and three departed to catch up on the events of the day.

Chapter 3

THE RELAXED BANTER
AND THE EPIPHANY

They reached El Camino Real and had to further go down the road to hook a U turn and park along the street in front of Bambino's, Harvey was happy that Devlin had chosen this place. Though it was along the busy highway, it was isolated. Next door was a liquor store and on the right was what appeared to be a shop for thong underwear with mannequins wearing that most desirable apparel. The right place to be, between wine and women.

Devlin led the way in and greeted the owner as a long lost friend, a huge character with a moustache, the moustache menacing, but more to hide a giant gap in his lip. They ordered beer and after ritual clicking of glasses, took satisfying swigs of the brew and settled down.

Devlin broke the silence, "its good we started before four thirty!"

36

Taggart and Harvey could not understand the significance, "Why?"

"That would have been Rahukala!" said Devlin and added "You can't start on a journey after the start of Rahukalam"

He had now before him two mystified colleagues, "Why Not?" they chorused.

"The malefic planet Rahu at the time is in full power and will thwart your purpose!".

Taggart snorted, "The last time I checked there is no rock around the sun called Rahu!"

Devlin was unfazed by the skepticism "It's a shadow planet; it's more malefic If it's retrograde".

Taggart was getting riled, "Retrograde means in retreat right? Boy! I would like my Captain to be in retrograde mode any time of day, anyway who gave you this shit?"

"My neighbor, she is deeply spiritual . . .", before Devlin could add further details of his eastern connection, Harvey intervened, he did not want this to become an acrimonious discussion on east versus west set of beliefs.

"Listen, let's set some of the things that we have found in order, it will help me write up the report for the chief, he'll expect that I will have one ready first thing in the morning. We started this morning with a lot of unknowns,"

Devlin stood up and started, "We have known knowns, we have some known unknowns, some unknown unknowns . . . ." Doing a fair good imitation of the Defense Secretary Rumsfeld.

Harvey & Taggart broke up in laughter; finally Harvey said "Will the Defense Secretary please yield to the speaker on the floor of the house"

Regaining his composure he started, "The professor was shot in his study and we know . . ." he held up a hand to stop Devlin from starting off again, "he was shot through the open window by some unknown . . ." again raising his hand hastily to finish his summary without breaking up into helpless laughter, "gunman, the killer most certainly entered the house and tried to strangle the already dead victim. The victim is way too wealthy than it appears at first glance, we don't know if it is illicit money, but we know that he paid his taxes honestly. We know that his wife thought that he was in some danger, what danger we don't know . . . ."

This mixture of knowns and unknowns was too much for Taggart and Devlin and they were grinning broadly.

Harvey too had to stop and resumed his summation "He was definitely selling his home, he had firm plans on moving away to Napa to a vineyard, he had lots of money, if the killer wanted to lay his hands on the money, a gunpoint holdup or kidnapping would have a better chance. The money was in the victims Bank or in the bank safe locker, the keys were in the desk, the killer did not search for it. Murder for gain is in all probability not the motive."

And he added thoughtfully, "the only person known to have access is a person, who was housekeeping for him out of sense of gratitude, not exactly the usual suspect".

The silence that ensued was broken by Taggart, "It was jealousy!" he said firmly and as he spoke his demeanor had changed as if his words were being guided by a spirit within, "It must have been envy of the most virulent kind, that drove that person to seek out and destroy the person who had what he himself couldn't possess, money?, No, it was something else that the victim had and the killer could not get".

The rest of the evening was spent in talking about everything but the investigation, finally Harvey stood up to go, "I better get home at least in time for dinner, as it is, I have committed the cardinal sin of missing quality family time on a Sunday, I don't know if Susan is going to roast me or put the ice age chill on me".

His frank confession of marital discord surprised the other two, who did not know him at all before this day. Harvey then paid for their evening to the surly moustache and outside Bambino's finding the liquor store open went in and got a bottle of scotch, telling himself that he might need that to dull the pain that most certainly awaited him at home.

Chapter 4

THE SEARCH AND THE LADDER

When Harvey arrived at his office in the morning he was in dark mood, as expected his return home last evening had not been good. Morning had brought no change and the house was like a radiation zone, too hot to endure very long. He drove to his office and decided to immerse himself in work to put the personal events out of his mind.

The Lieutenant of Major Crimes, his immediate boss was waiting for him, Harvey launched into the events of yesterday, he left nothing out, and Lieutenant Jim Boskey was known to be good boss, but very exacting and did not tolerate sloppy work. When Harvey finished, Boskey shot him just one question, "This woman who called it in, you sent her home without a formal statement?"

"Yes, but I did not think she could be involved except in finding the body". Harvey was defensive but not defiant, "I am going to call her now to get that statement".

Boskey did not seem convinced with his reply, "You do just that right now, but I can tell you the prosecution office will not be happy to find this out, even if you catch the guy who did this and dig up the evidence to nail him, the defense attorney will put you on the stand and say Oh!, so the only person known to have access to the house was let go without questioning?, who knows what she then did to plant evidence to implicate my client. The prosecution case will fold right there. I can tell you that your investigation is compromised right now less than 24 hours after starting. I don't have to tell you to keep in mind the standard that is required here, Beyond Reasonable Doubt, so from now on do things by the book and don't let personal judgment get in the way of closing this case".

Harvey was stunned by the last shot from the Lieut., personal judgment? Like in personal bias? He hoped that it was a choice of words that didn't apply to his treatment of Elle.

He called Elle and found her at home, she said that the office had called and asked her to take a few days off, they were aware of her ties to Prof. Dennis McPherson. She readily agreed to come in about half hour and give her statement.

Harvey was determined to make amends for his display of gallantry last night. He would be as impersonal as a homicide investigator could be.

Taggart and Devlin made their appearance, a first for them at the Sheriff's headquarters. They seemed impressed, the Major Crime Unit occupied an entire floor and apart from the detective's stations, there were Forensic Specialists, Crime Analysts, and so many others, the atmosphere was electric, energy seemed to flow around the activities here. Compared to this their San Carlos PD was an out post-a confidence building mechanism than an action station.

Devlin's enthusiasm was evident and Taggart also seemed keen to get into action. Taggart seeing first hand a murder investigation and particularly Harvey's complete immersion at the crime scene yesterday had fired his imagination.

For Harvey this was a much needed boost, it lifted the gloom in which he had begun the day.

He quickly assigned them the morning tasks, Taggart was to follow up on the Agency that carried out the contract on the Creeper and the painting, collecting as much detail as possible of the workmen who had been at the worksite since the previous week.

Devlin was to head to University and meet the faculty at the professors department and look up any known associates there. He was about to add a word of caution to moderate Devlin's approach who would be dealing with academicians. The kind he presumed lived in a rarefied universe of their own specialty and to whom the intrusion of real world police work causes alarm. But Harvey decided that he could give the benefit of doubt to the young fresh faced policeman to deal with due deference to the faculty at the university. The faculty could be vocal and voluble and if a popular professor termed the killing as a failure of intelligence on the part of the Sheriff's office there would be uproar. Never mind that there had been no murders in San Carlos in the last six years, the media starved for details in the case had picked up on the fact that he had been shot gangland style. It was bad PR to portray San Carlos as a place where gun toting gang members shot up peaceful citizens.

The chief was clever and had embarked on a PR exercise to recruit volunteers to his office, his reasoning that the volunteers would feel as part of the police and less likely to indulge in anti-social activities. So there were about 200 of these wannabee police, there was of course a need to find some police work for them to keep them engaged, the chief's favorite involved launching searches for missing children, so even if a child had been missing for a year a search was launched in the hills to the west of the city. The danger of coming across mountain lions added some thrill to the often futile treks of the volunteers.

The two San Carlos Cops then went out, having made plans to get back together late afternoon at headquarters.

He sat down at his station and began to type up his report; he did this rapidly and without sweating it out as others did. It came easily to him, he prided himself on organizing his thoughts and putting them down on paper was no big deal. It was approaching the time for his meet with Elle and he hastened to complete the job at hand. As he finished he felt the weight of the pouch given to him by the crime scene crewman last night. The key were heavy and had pulled at his jacket in constant reminder.

He quickly left his work station and went up to the Lieut's office, knocked and entered, "Chief, the crime lab people found some bunch of bank locker keys and gave them to me, can I go in without a warrant?".

Lieut. Boskey seemed astounded by this, after a moment he asked slowly as if speaking to a dull student, "The Crime lab people handed over some evidence to you at the scene?"

Harvey's response was as casual as he could manage, "Yes" and from his jacket dug out the pouch and it jangled with the keys inside, mentally the palm of his hand had flown and landed on his brow as soon as he realized the cardinal sin in evidentiary custody rule, Unauthorized Possession. Possession, outside the log of the system collecting and tracking the items at every stage.

Though he could not imagine how a defense counsel would use that in a trial, Boskey clearly did not have any doubt as to the extent of damage.

Boskey seemed to make up his mind, "All right, you hit the banks today, but before that, come back here, I will have a letter ready from me endorsed by the

Mayor, she's no babe in the woods, I might be able to persuade her that it is good intercity relations, that we are helping in quick resolution of a San Carlos tragedy, the letter will at least establish that a rouge detective is not digging around private financial records of citizens, BUT make sure you have a Crime lab guy who logs in everything that you find, this is not a reflection on your honesty but, hell, I am going out on a limb to stand by you.".

Harvey, politically neutral, didn't care if the mayor wanted to garner some votes.

Harvey nodded gratefully and headed back to his station and found a message that Elle was waiting in the lobby, he asked that she be taken to the interrogation rooms on the 5th floor and went there down himself.

The interrogation rooms here was special. It protected the officers who were discharging their duties lawfully, first of all it was all wired for sound, the CC TV cameras had no blind spots. The previous chief had insisted that the name be changed to "Interview rooms" and accordingly the sign boards changed, but little else.

Harvey greeted Elle warmly and asked if she wanted something to drink and offered her a cappuccino, telling her that the Sheriff's office had moved up the lifestyle quotient and the cafeteria was upgraded to a formal restaurant. In fact there had been spirited bidding to win the tender floated to run the restaurant and the mayor deciding the issue in favor of a popular local outfit. It was not narrow political consideration but more like, Think Global, Act Local or some such. The successful bidder realizing the potential of hungry hordes of law enforcement personnel had exceeded expectations.

Harvey was aware that his every word was being recorded and that his solicitous manner toward a deponent could touch of a speculation. He didn't care if the entire detective squad gossiped about his soft spot for Elle.

He started the interview quite formally and kept his questions to a minimum letting her narrate the events of yesterday. Her narration did not add anything to the report that he had already written up. Then he briefly questioned her about her relationship to the family. She spoke warmly of the deceased and the other two members of the family, choking a bit at recalling the kindness of the man who was her savior and mentor. Harvey then switched to questions on the Professors' circle of friends and visitors to the office, was she aware of any threat or danger that he faced? When had the professor decide to move away from San Carlos, did she know the reason? Did his wife ever mention to Elle that she was afraid for his safety? Elle said that she was completely unaware of any such thing. Life was normal; Life was good the only thing that bothered her was the family move from San Carlos to Napa Valley, where she could not move because of her job.

Harvey then left her to confer with Boskey, wanted to know if the lieutenant had any new line of questioning to be done. Boskey shook his head and said that she appeared straight, adding that Harvey had done a good and proper interview. Having chewed out Harvey twice since the morning, Boskey felt he needed a pat on the back, need to keep up the morale of troops you know, part of his man management, inter personal skills they called it.

Having finished the interview, Harvey escorted Elle out of the building, she said it was OK she would find her way but Harvey insisted and outside he watched her get into the car and drive away, he stood for a while soaking in the early winter sun and taking a break from the intense work since the morning.

As promised the Lieutenant had got his authorization letter endorsed by the Mayor, the titular head of the city. Harvey then fished out the keys from the pouch and all the keys were helpfully tagged with the Bank's name. He then drove to the nearest and formally presenting the authorization letter asked the bank manager to allow him access to the lockers.

The manager inclined to cooperate asked Harvey doubtfully, "Shouldn't this be a court order?"

Harvey patiently explained that it was a murder investigation and there were no issues of invasion of privacy and in the absence of next-of-kin there was no one to ask for permission, in any event the exigencies of the moment required speed to get to the truth.

The Manager then escorted him down to the basement and opened the vault and opened the locker first with his master key and then Harvey used the one from the pouch. The locker was not large, about twice the size of a normal desk drawer, inside there were papers, bunches of them tied together. Harvey pulled out a few and took them to a table and opened the strings and noted they were financial records, the dead man's record of money remitted to various banks, the details of his tax filings. Letters from his CPA that appeared printed from e mails. There was a lot of money involved. This could take days, if not weeks to appraise the total involved. Harvey read a few of the e-mail print out from the CPA, a Mr. Jonathan Philer. Harvey jotted down the details of his contact and made a note to call on him for questioning. But what, apart from the financial side, would an accountant know, why his client was killed in the prime of his life. Harvey mused that murder investigation was like a maze; you entered an opening, came upon a dead end and retraced your steps to find a way out.

Then something caught his eye, the remittances were all from some companies and they all appeared to be in Nevada. He looked at the names and tried to recall if he had heard of them before, one was prominent and he knew that company owned a hotel and casino in Las Vegas.

Casino sending money to a professor? That puzzled him a lot. This would require a closer look and for the first time since the start of this probe missed his partner. Megan Jones, she of the bright eyes and booming voice was on maternity leave close to half year. No other detective was assigned as his partner. The fifteen other detectives were already paired together and were like married couple, squabbling but loyal to each other. He and Megan had been mostly dealing with cold case files and a few serious assault cases so it was felt by the administration that he cope with it alone. Harvey speculated that San Francisco homicide squads were up to their ears in murder cases, but much of San Mateo County had been sanitized by the tech money in the valley.

Casino, money and the Professor the three were linked together somehow, his search had established that much, he then recalled what the crime scene crew had said last evening, the professors computer had a live feed from a casino table. Is it possible, Harvey asked himself, that the Professor was a compulsive on line Gambler and that he had hit upon a sure shot way of taking away a lot of Casino money? Maybe the Casinos found out about his scam and sent in their hit man. But Casinos did not wire money to winner's bank accounts, or did they? Harvey did not know, he would find out.

Following the Lieutenant Boskey's advice he called the Crime Lab to send in someone to pick the documents that he had in this locker and log it in, plus, Harvey would have additional help in deciphering the data contained in them, the center had recently added a team for financial forensics. He had heard them boast that it was more complicated than simple murder and required analytics. What did they do? Autopsy the accounts?

The document man from the crime lab arrived, he was the same geek looking guy who had been at the house yesterday, he had been sorting out the papers found in the desk and now the prospect of a treasure trove of papers in the locker of a dead man was highly promising. They made a log of the papers found in the locker and the list was presented to the Bank Manager for his signature. The Bank Manager was reluctant, he did not want to sign papers that he did not understand, and he did overcome his diffidence and signed, wondering if the estate of a slain customer could sue him and the bank for invasion of privacy, violating client confidentiality and damages for causing emotional distress by the disclosure. He supposed they could, given the way the law was working in this law abiding country. He confided his fears to Harvey, who sympathetically narrated how a friend was fined for shooting a deer and wounding it, he had not known that hunting a deer and not killing it was a crime!, wrong ammunition, some law!. The bank manager shuffled back to his cabin even more depressed.

Harvey exited the bank and was surprised to see it getting dark, he had lost track of time in the windowless Locker room, another bank was around the corner and he decided to walk there. Inside he repeated his exigencies of investigation and this manager led him to the lockers without fuss. The locker when he opened it had Harvey gaping, the manager whose curiosity was piqued looked over his shoulder and he too gaped. The locker was stacked with money, piles of it, neatly banded and fresh off the press. The locker was bigger than the one at the other bank; Harvey's guesstimate was that it would be close to 5 to 10 million bucks. Hard to be sure, but a four foot pile of moolah had to amount at least that much. He shut the locker door firmly, deciding that seeing was enough, and it would in no way help in the investigation. They say Money Talks, he would beg to differ. Finding the money in his search did not tell him anything. All this loot could well have been covered by the huge taxes that he seemed to have paid. The holy grail for prosecuting Tax evasion was the money trail, remittances was what the IRS man looked for, not piles of green backs. The Tax payer could always claim that having paid his taxes, he hoarded cash for a rainy day, who didn't like hard cash?

As he stepped out of the bank a Ferrari flashed down the road, his thoughts veered around to Susan, his wife lately found it fun to disparage everything about him, she stuck a bumper sticker on his car that said "I want to grow up and be a Beemer". May be he should get a BMW even if it was only at the used car lot, spruce it up and turn the odometer back to show less mileage. He wondered if an electronic odometer could be turned back, technology complicated a lot of simple dreams. The cell phone in his pocket chirped pulling him back from the abyss that he was in danger of slipping into.

It was Taggart calling suppressing the excitement in his voice, he had been to visit agency that cut down the tree and painted the house. The story was that the business was run by an elderly pair of brothers, when they had finished the job last week the client asked them to leave the ladder behind and he would pay for it and he needed one around the house. So they did, but on Saturday one of the Lee brothers got a call asking them to take it away, they did not know who the caller was, who insisted that they remove the ladder that very day. So they sent one of their crew to retrieve it, the young lad had stopped by late on Saturday and had dismantled it to fit in his truck. Taggart had managed to talk to that workman, who said that there was no one when he went in to get it, he was there for a while to separate the two sections, loaded up in the truck and left. The one inescapable conclusion was that the murderer had called to have the ladder removed. Find that caller and they would find the killer.

Taggart also said that Devlin had called from the University and had found nothing significant except that the Professor maintained a small apartment over at University Terraces that actually was meant for students. As the hour was late, they changed the plan to meet that evening at headquarters and meet and plan the next course of action in the morning.

But having called off the meeting with his deputies, Harvey was loath to go home, he thought of his absent partner Megan and called her and she happily called him over.

How he missed her now when he badly needed someone to be by his side and make him laugh and forget his home situation. He had read in the newspapers that some had said that Pakistan is the place you send your mother-in-law to, now that his mother-in-law had arrived for the season his house was

Pakistan. The mother and daughter combo was deadlier than a suicide bomber. Maybe not deadlier but certainly more painful, you got struck by verbal shrapnel, Post Traumatic Stress Disorder never too far away.

Megan's husband warmly welcomed him and handed him a drink, Megan announced that a felony was in progress in the Kitchen with Jacob drowning the spaghetti in super spicy sauce. She claimed that Jacob made it so that it kept her awake at night and mind the baby while he avoided eating his own cooking and slept like a baby.

Harvey relaxed in the jovial air in the house, Megan did ask him why he had pulled the duty on the homicide and not Joey&Joey, a pair of detectives who were fast tracking their careers and grabbed just about any assignment that would bring them career glory and a promotion. Harvey told her that Lieutenant Bosky had called him and asked to take it and had remarked that it would take his mind off other things, which meant the status of his married life. That meant that his situation was common knowledge in the department. He then asked quite timidly if Megan was ready to resume her work, Jacob said "Of course, she is chomping at the bit to get back to work". Megan turned on him "What, now I look like a filly to you?" Her ready wit was always a pleasure for Harvey and he was happy when she said that just that morning she had called the chief and wanted to get back to duty. They paired well, while he looked to gain insight, her broad outlook cleared a lot of cobwebs around the crime scenes.

Chapter 5

THE SECRETS OF THE MONEY

Harvey woke up and dressed hurriedly, there had been a call saying the McPherson family, Wife and son, had arrived and wanted to see the dearly departed. He chose his best dark suit. He knew well the trauma that loved ones had to undergo to come in and identify a murdered man and the red tape that always distressed them. So he called the people at the morgue and asked them to prepare for the visit and ensure that the family was not put out unduly having to deal with the Coroner's office and the inevitable paper work. Tilden himself promised to be present and guide them. As he came downstairs he found his wife and mother-in-law having breakfast and Susan seeing him dressed in his best said "We are going to a wedding are we?" "Or a funeral" added his Mom-in-law. He did not respond and hurried out of his personal Pakistan.

At the city morgue he was surprised to see a large number of people milling around the entrance, he had been expecting only the wife & son. It seemed that friends had accompanied them for support. Many were of the son David's age, others older. And they were a dignified lot and conversed in whispers. Harvey spotted Elle standing with a lady he presumed to be the wife of the dead Professor, Elle made the introductions. Miriam was a woman of exceptional beauty and carried herself with a quiet dignity and poise. A young man joined them, again Elle made the introduction, David had the easy grace of an athlete and seemed concerned for his mother. No doubt they had talked on the long flight home and drawn solace from each other. Harvey was sincere in his condolences to her and the son escorted them inside.

Tilden wore a mournful expression, quite a change from the normal scowl with which he greeted strangers. Miriam choked back a sob on seeing her husband of so many years lying lifeless on the table. Tilden told her that the end had been quick and the professor had not suffered in anyway. Tilden swung into action and got them through the paper work with a minimum of fuss and said they could shift the body to a funeral parlor and the coroner would be holding the inquest later that week.

As they exited the morgue, Harvey noted that the friends that accompanied them gathered around comforting the bereaved family. The Professor had been celebrated in life and now was mourned in death. The family had evidently built up loyal circle of friends testifying to a generous spirit and warmth. He wanted to ask Miriam about her remark to Elle about the danger that the professor faced, but having seen her distress he decided to wait for now, he had equally important tasks at hand.

He then hurried to the Sheriff's headquarters where he wanted to get to work immediately. For two days he had driven himself with commitment to moral duty, now it was fortified by a steely resolve to bring to justice the perpetrator of this crime.

At the Sheriff's HQ as he came out of the elevator, he came upon the wild welcome that Megan was accorded by the Major Crimes Unit on her return to duty, there she stood in the center of the Unit greeting everyone with the nicknames that she had generously bestowed on them, some cringed, others roared in laughter at her so apt characterizations. For all her jovial nature Megan was not be trifled with, once Harvey remembered, a fellow officer compared the two them to Elephant and the Mahout, a snide remark at her girth and his lean frame, Megan at that time gave no indication that she had heard the remark. In the days that followed, she targeted that fellow to a barrage of jokes, witty one liners that was bang on target every time, There were no come backs from that fellow, it became a daily ritual and the entire unit would wait for the morning jibe from Megan and they would roar with laughter. The poor fellow had no place to hide, he dreaded coming into the office. The final straw came when he badly flubbed a briefing in front of the entire unit, Megan cheerfully suggested "Will someone give this guy a Webster's?", that did it, he sought and got a transfer to correctional unit where he had to deal with felons, better to deal with Felons on the mend, than this.

Harvey enjoyed the celebrations of Megan's 'Home coming' for a while, then called his team together,

Lieutenant Bosky stepped out of the office and indicated that he wanted to be present for the review of the case, they moved on to the briefing room.

Harvey recounted his findings at the bank, the documents of finance at the first locker and the huge hard cash hoard in the second locker, his belief that the Casino companies were paying the Professor a lot of money for whatever reasons and that it appeared to be going for some time. He needed to talk to the professor's CPA on his Income Sources, Tax filing etc. Maybe talk to the casino companies also. Nobody offered a suggestion why the casinos' paid him.

Taggart then recounted his findings of the previous day, the agency involved in the painting, the ladder being removed from the site on late Saturday, the phone call asking for the ladder be removed.

This represented the best lead in the case so far, find the caller and find the murderer. They needed to trace the call and the phone used to make the call. They discussed the issue, Taggart who had not done this before asked if he could go to the phone service provider to Lee Brothers and get the call details, did he need a warrant from a judge?.

Lieutenant Bosky put him at ease, "No you go there and ask for it, they have to cooperate with Law Enforcement, it's the law now, Homeland Security made sure of that rule with the phone companies. In any case I will call them, just tell me the service providers name".

Taggart fished out a paper from his jacket and gave it to Bosky, "This is an invoice from the phone company over in Burlingame that I picked up". Harvey was happy that Taggart had shown foresight, Taggart's next stop would be that service provider.

But before they could move on, the youngest member Devlin had a question, "What if it is throw away phone, a prepaid one that he makes that one call from and throws it away?

Lieutenant Bosky shook his head, "Even prepaid phones now have safeguards, after you buy one the service provider has to call that phone and give the number at which point some identity is required"

He hadn't dismissed the young cop's question, but wanted to keep him interested in the hunt, he said, "second to activate the account for the amount paid, you would have to ring the call center, again some identity has to be given" Bosky paused thoughtfully, "A smart man may do that, give a false ID and get a prepaid, but that requires forethought, you have to have an alternate identity ready"

He then turned over in his mind the sequence of events that had been reconstructed so far and said "it is not a spur of the moment decision to get one, at least not in this case, I don't think so, the culprit seeing the ladder and wanting it removed, didn't go out and get a throw away phone and then make that call, I bet he had the phone with him".

Taggart did not want to wait any longer; he strode out of the briefing room at a brisk pace promising to call them as soon as he found something of the phone call at the phone service provider.

Devlin began the briefing of his work yesterday at the University, he told them of the people he had met, the faculty, the students, and the office staff. The gist of the findings: it appeared that the Late Professor was loved universally. All had a good word to say about him. Great teacher, friendly, kind to the non-academic and support staff etc. etc. No one appeared to bear any ill will towards him nor did anyone suggest that someone resented him in any way. As he continued it was clear that Devlin had done a job as thoroughly as possible of canvassing the Professor's work place. Devlin sensed that his narrative showed no progress in aiding the investigation.

To cut short, he said that the professor was active in both the mathematics and Statistics. While the faculty in the Math department had been very cooperative, in the Statistics department he had come upon a Professor, called Dr. Brandon Murphy, who he had been told, was closest to Professor McPherson. But Dr. Murphy after initially answering questions had turned nasty and made some truly nasty cracks about the police. He had taunted Devlin about not finding a single witness to even hearing a gun shot in a quiet neighborhood. Devlin had maintained his composure but the man went on with his diatribe.

The last thing that Dr. Murphy said to him struck him as odd and he repeated it, "That man should have spent his money in paying for private protection than to rely on the local police".

Devlin said that he quickly asked him "Were you aware of any danger to Professor McPherson?"

"Ah! Danger!" the professor had said "Everyone lives dangerously, anybody can get shot, and everybody has got guns now". So was he against guns?

Dr. Murphy began laughing uproariously "No! No!, I would give it away free in Iraq, Afghanistan or Pakistan, great big bazookas not piddly rifles. Give it to them free, by the shipload. It will give a new meaning to Gunboat Diplomacy!"

The three others in the briefing room having listened to this, exchanged looks, Boskey knowing Harvey's focus on finding a dark character capable of murder said to him, "You have your first candidate". Harvey focused now on the words spoken by Dr. Murphy, MONEY, and PRIVATE PROTECTION.

The first pointed to knowledge of Professor's Money, was he aware that he got money from sources other than the University?

The second thing that he had said implied there was some danger, a threat? Why did a colleague imagine such a thing? Did he know anything?

Devlin recounting of the professor's bizarre behavior coupled with indications of his views or may be of his knowledge made him a possible candidate. Dr. Murphy would now become the focus of the investigation. Next he would have to turn to the evidence, search and collate details and build the circumstantial evidence.

So far they had not come across the possibility of an eye witness; they would have to build the case on circumstantial evidence. In the best of circumstances such evidence was hard to come by and second, using it in securing prosecution quite another thing. Given the very technical nature of the evidence, prosecutors preferred that such cases be tried by a Judge and not a jury. The defense invariably plumped for trial by jury and refused to waive that right. They alone could exercise that right. Circumstantial evidence was not only hard to come by and so they had to look harder. Harvey likened it to picking lint, you looked, there it was and a closer look found one more, piece by piece, the only thing here was that you couldn't use a brush to do a faster job.

Harvey walked up to the white board and began to mark out a timeline. The timeline imposed restrictions, events that could have happened in particular time limit, events that could not have happened and so on. They could seek alibi of suspects. It also narrowed things, sometimes to the advantage of the Investigating team. He drew a line on top beginning with Noon of Saturday the day the of the professors death. Below that he drew a long line downward right up to the bottom of the board. On that line he made sections, one section was the time of death; they would get the proximate time of death from Tilden. The Autopsy would indicate an interval of time going back from the time of discovery to the possible earliest time of death.

But right now he placed it at three in the afternoon, and on a parallel line the time of discovery was known. Without pause he swiftly marked the time of call to the painting contractor, the probable time of the arrival of the workman to pick up the ladder, the interval that the youngster had in dismantling the ladder and it loading his truck before leaving.

Boskey, Megan and Devlin marveled at the fluency with which Harvey made the markings, showing that his thinking was organized and he had mentally collated the details which he now transferred to the timeline on the Board. Below the line for the discovery of the crime, the details were sparse, the return of the wife and son marked tentatively. There was in fact no event after the discovery of the body that could be seen as a link to the murder.

So there was the box, a time starting possibly at three of Saturday and at 7.30 on Sunday morning. In that box they had to fit in a suspect. His presence, the likelihood of his presence, anything physical at the crime scene evidence (fingerprints ruled out), DNA could take time, if they could match with a sample. As for Dr. Murphy, they could question him as to where he was at the time but before that they had to have some link, some way to tie him to the murder as a possible suspect. They had zilch!

At that moment when Dr. Murphy loomed large in their thoughts, Taggart excited, called from the phone service provider's office and that changed everything.

Chapter 6

THE OPEN AND SHUT CASE

When Taggart called they felt that he had left them just moments age, either that or they had lost track of time or that Taggart had sped to his destination with the lights flashing and sirens blaring. Actually it was nearly two hours since Taggart had left on his quest, Taggart had indeed sped north with the sirens on. Arriving at his destination he realized that the service provider was located right behind Lee Brother's business. The phone company took his request and, no fuss, produced a print out of all call received and made from Lee Brothers during the last 10 days. The numbers making no sense to Taggart, he went into meet the elderly brothers and asked them to focus on any numbers that they did not recognize at the approximate time of the call received asking them to take away their ladder. This they did and the numbers were narrowed down to five.

Taggart hot footed it back to the phone company and this time he got the answer, four of the numbers did not check out but the fifth was an International number, the phone company manager made a few calls and then told him, the phone is an India registered phone with an International Roaming facility. The billing and call records would be with the service provider in India and then he offered to help and called India, explaining to Taggart that it was little past midnight in India. But, wonders never cease, the world of business was now 24X7, and he had a response and the list of Calls from that phone was sent to him. Taggart took the print out and was shaken, the phone was in the name of DAVID McPherson, the son. The last call made was to the Lee Brothers business.

At HQ, there was stunned silence when David's name came on the speaker phone. Harvey had a pained expression on his face. The disclosure was a negation of his opinion; it hurt his self-belief in the ability to judging people. But he picked himself up and gestured to Megan telling Boskey, "I will go talk to them both right now".

Boskey did not agree, "Call them here I want to be there when you talk to that boy, he better come clean".

Boskey was legendary in interrogating suspects, one look at him and most of the suspects changed from defiance to outright surrender. They might not blabber a confession but quickly changed their pleas to Guilty, this was often against the advice of counsel. Copping a guilty plea was no guarantee that they would not wind up serving time. Sentenced to serving time the convict was advised that he could file an Appeal, in the plea to the Appeal Court they went with "inadequate representation of counsel", a valid ground to challenge conviction. The system took care of it, the Appeal courts agreeing with the appeal that there had been inadequate representation of counsel reversed the order of conviction by the lower court, but hold your breath, reverted the matter to the lower court for the fresh consideration of the accused that his confession should not have been admitted as evidence, now a new defense counsel took up the matter. The appeals and cross appeals kept the court system busy, In the meanwhile the convict effectively served out his sentence,

The score card in the legal battle: People Vs. Felons, 2-1,

Boskey 's reputation was sealed when a defense attorney trying to get his client's confession ruled as "Inadmissible", pointed to Boskey's presence at the time of confession and said that the confession was under duress. After vigorous protests from prosecutors that any third degree was used, the attorney said, "Your Honor I didn't say that third degree was used, but look at that face", pointing to Boskey he pleaded, "that is the face of wrath of Justice and my client helplessly succumbed to it".

The "wrath of Justice" look was on Boskey's face and Harvey didn't fight it, Megan patted his back and he sat back down. Megan would be the lead interrogator it was decided and she began to jot down the possible line of questions.

Harvey made the call and politely asked that they come in to the Sheriff's HQ for a formal statement. They agreed readily and set the time at 2.30 in the afternoon explaining that there were people in the house. It took a moment for Harvey to realize that since his call to Tilden, asking that Tilden and the staff at the city morgue to be as helpful to the family as possible, he had declared the house in Easton Villas as no longer a crime scene. So he was directly responsible for the family to get into the house even before they had a suspect. That suspect could be the son.

First they sent Devlin to talk to the CPA of the dead don, the name that had cropped up in the papers found in the bank locker, a fool's errand, how much ever you may love your team the need to effectively deploy your force was supreme.

Harvey and Mega had an hour to wait for McPhersons to come in; they decided to go down to have lunch. As they neared the elevator, one half of the Joey&Joey team stepped out with a big box of Krispy Kreme doughnuts. Megan spotting an opportunity was effusive in greeting the detective.

"Hey, Joey, Howdy, what have you got here, glazed doughnuts? You sure know your way to a lady's heart" patting his back heartily. They neatly relieved him of the burden and helped themselves at a desk. Harvey didn't feel the least bit guilty, a little sinful yes, but not guilty. They were guilty though of ignoring the ban on food at the unit, HQ had imposed the ban after a rodent problem was reported in the building. Nobody had actually seen rats running around, but it was bad for the image if it was known there were rats in Law enforcement! The sheriff was concerned that any report in the media on his office would begin with the descriptive, "At the rat infested HQ of the county sheriff . . . ."

Harvey was in a much better mood when he went down with Megan to await the arrival of Miriam and David. When they came in Harvey was surprised to see Elle accompanying them. She was not expected nor called to be present. Harvey told her, "This could take a while; you will bored waiting here why don't you go around to the city library?"

This was the equivalent of shouting "Take a Hike!" Elle turned around sharply and walked away. The women, Miriam and Megan sensitive to such things, noted the sudden regret in Harvey's eye.

Diplomatically separating the mother and son, Harvey led Miriam to one room and Megan took David to another. Harvey knew that Boskey would be viewing the interviews in both rooms on the other side of the one way mirrors. Something about the fact that people are watching you silently tends to inhibit people under such scrutiny, Miriam did seem at ease but Harvey knew she would be circumspect due to just that reason.

Miriam began her narrative with the call from Elle telling her of the death of her husband, her subsequent efforts to contact her son who was in a remote part of the country. Unable to reach him after trying, she decided to send him an e mail and booked her passage to San Francisco via Hong Kong the fastest way to get back and how when she reached Chennai on the East Coast to catch her flight she was met by her son at the airport who said he got the e mail and rushed to join her.

Harvey then without any preliminaries asked her about her saying to Elle that she knew it was dangerous, what was the danger that she knew about?

"Yes, I always associated gambling with crime, all that easy money lure. Where there is so much money then crime comes into it. Dennis also used to think that it was bound to create dangerous situations and when I heard that he had been shot my first thought was that it had to do with his work for the casinos".

"So, you didn't know of any specific threat or danger that he faced?" Harvey asked, hoping for a big break in investigation.

"Yes, I mean no, I don't know of any specific danger that he was in, but my fears had increased after all that cash came in from Las Vegas last year. Even Dennis felt uncomfortable with it and he had told me that he was going to stop his consultancy with them, he also told me vaguely that corruption comes into the system when insiders get greedy"

Harvey had been bothered about the Professors work for the casinos ever since his visit to the bank lockers, "What was he consulting about for the Casinos?"

Miriam astonished him with a short answer, "Security".

Security? What's a mathematics professor got to do with security? You associated security with guys packing guns, not professors with laser pointers in University halls.

Seeing his bewildered expression she clarified, "Not physical security, business safety and viability, he provided them solutions to operate the casinos with a more secure margin, it had to do with his work on probability".

He was still mystified by any role that the professor had played in gambling, "How did he get into it? And what did he do for them?"

"It began while we were on a cruise and landed in Macau, that's a great gambling destination" Harvey nodded he had read about Macau, a former Portuguese colony becoming a major gambling destination, rivaling the status of Las Vegas. In fact there had been mournful reportage in the business papers that the West had ceded one more position of being numero uno in the world to the resurgent East. This rise of Macau as the number one gambling center was in keeping with the change in world order. It was 'the Asian Century'.

Miriam began her narrative, it was not a structured story, he could sense that she was reliving the time in the past of the events that ultimately led to the death of her husband, that carefree past had somehow through twists and turns had put her husband in the path of danger. The dangers that she had only vaguely perceived, if she had but sensed the need to react to those dangers perhaps the tragedy would not have been the outcome. Ultimately what had begun as a holiday indulgence propelled her husband on a second career. A dual life that brought them meaningless riches and cast him as an adversary of a cold blooded killer.

"Dennis played for some time and then he became excited saying he knew to beat the system and over the next 2 days spent all his time at the tables and made a lot of money, in fact that winning paid for half our cruise"

"When we returned stateside he started to visit Las Vegas and as always made good money, I think that after a few visits, the casino people started to notice the consistent winning and called him in, they keep tabs on those who come in with all sorts of schemes to cheat the casinos and he was one such. But he told them frankly that they were allowing him to win because the system had weaknesses. The upshot of the whole thing was, he offered to fix things for them in such a way that the machine did not pay out more than a certain percentage. At that time the casinos were hurting badly, not that they were losing money, but the operating margins are very thin and the games are designed to pay out at least 75% as winnings, that's the law in Nevada, but the casinos were actually losing additional 10% or so and could not figure out a way to avoid that and so now he fixed the machines for them and they have paid him ever since"

All this sounded vaguely illicit to Harvey and he asked her as much, "Is it not illegal to do that with the machines?"

"Oh yes! They can send you to prison for six years!" This frank admission of criminal activity astonished Harvey whose eyebrows rose to meet his hairline.

Miriam started to laugh at his expression "No, Dennis wasn't doing anything illegal; he said the machines work that way because he understood the paradox".

Harvey continued to be puzzled "What paradox?"

"Don't ask me, I know as much as you do" she corrected herself "I mean as much as the next person, Dennis tried to explain a few times, basically it has to do with outcomes expected, If a question is asked in such a way, any which you answer would appear contradictory, that would be a paradox in logic, similarly in numbers theory Dennis said that a Paradox alters the outcome in a probability situation, *if one understands the contradiction*, whatever that means. Which I presumed applied to games of chance, such as Gambling, other than that I don't know what else"

Harvey had now a measure of understanding that McPherson used his knowledge of Mathematics to help casinos in a business way and they paid him, no criminal enterprise there; his death may not be connected in anyway with all that money.

Miriam tried to dispel any lingering notion in his mind that Dennis indulged in crime "What Dennis did was all above board, he designed game machines and logic so that it confirmed to laws on gambling, the law is very rigorous in Nevada, they have standards for the machines and a rigorous certification before the Casino can put up a game. They are field tested and certified that it is not manipulated, they have to pay out at least 75% of the wagers on that machine. Dennis made sure that they did not pay out MORE than that. To test the machine they literally tear apart the machine and test the software. Dennis once travelled to Slovenia to understand the testing process; there they have very high skills in testing such machines particularly the mathematical skills and understanding of randomness"

With all the information that he had gathered in this interview, Harvey felt that made some progress in his understanding of complexities in human activity, as for the advancement of his investigation nothing at all, Zero. The result of this interview a nullity, to put it in proper scientific terms, thought Harvey ruefully.

In the other interview room, the faceoff between Megan and David began and things changed rapidly, in fact within the first five minutes of beginning.

Megan did not begin with a ritualistic "sorry for the loss of your father in tragic circumstances" there would be no expressions of regrets to the bereaved son.

She shot her first question "Where were you on the night of October 28, Saturday" "In India" David all wide eyed innocence, he actually raised a hand and pointed at the window.

Megan was tempted to follow the direction of his finger and barking and demanding "Where?" That would certainly unsettle him. Not that she expected him to get so unsettled as to jump to his feet and confess "Yes! I shot the bastard right between his eyes"

But keep him off balance and chances are that his answer would come, not that well prepared and create an opening for a clear probe and arrive at the truth.

"When did you return from India?" "I arrived past midnight this Sunday, no Monday he corrected himself, I came back with my mother you can ask her" again his hand pointing vaguely in the direction of the door. The guy WAS unsettled!

"I am asking you!" no let up from his adversary. "Who told you that your father had been murdered?"

"Actually no one" David was sticking to actuals. "What? Then how did you know of his death?"

"I had an email from my mother" facts are facts.

But Megan was not done with him yet, "Why didn't she just call you?"

"I was deep in a cave, cell phones don't work there"

"Why were you in a cave?" her tone suggesting that Caves were not good places to be in.

"Studying ancient paintings, you know Ajanta & Ellora?"

Megan did not know, but she was tempted to ask him If it was erotic art, otherwise why would anyone go into a cave to see a painting? To her the question was quite legitimate; there must be a lot of erotic stuff there, ancient or otherwise, for them to relentlessly produce a billion souls.

Mercifully for him she shifted her question to cell phones, "Do you own a cell phone bought in India with international roaming facility?" David seemed to relax, "Yes". Confession at last! At least it was an admission of undeniable fact.

"Where is it now?"

"It will be in my father's study" this answer came with some assurance from him.

"Why would your cell phone be in your father's study?"

"In the summer when I came home I brought that phone, but forgot to take it back on my return, Dad used it to call me, he was tickled that I had to pay for his calls, so I kept the phone active and paid up the bills and got a new phone for myself in India, So that's how my phone is in my father's study" neatly summing up the situation.

Megan came to the sudden realization that this guy could not be possibly be a suspect. In fact he did not have a right to grace this building. That privilege was reserved for Cops, felons and prospective felons. Lawyers, except those from the prosecutor's office, were classified in the last category, all cops felt that way and she was not going to be the one to betray the fraternity.

It ended her much anticipated confrontation with a possible perpetrator. It saddened her, OPEN & SHUT CASE, she told herself, except that this had an unexpected ending.

Chapter 7

FOLLOW THE MONEY

The next morning when they met they were a dispirited lot, their one lead had petered out, one possible suspect turned out to be pure as the driven snow. They resolutely struck to the task at hand and decided to do a review of the interviews, if they had missed anything, a relook may bring up some ideas.

Megan interview being the shorter one went first. The replay was a perfect parody of a tough interrogation; it put them all in good humor. At one point Megan paused the tape and laughingly told them that when David said that he was in a cave looking at paintings, she had been tempted to ask if it was erotic art! As they laughed, she justified herself saying that there was possibly a lot of eroticism there looking at the billion plus people. They laughed harder, then she delivered the punch line, "Wonder what they all do if they get free time?" This time the room erupted in an uproar. The rest of the Unit outside the briefing room wondered what caused the uproar even when Chief Boskey was in there. Open and shut case they agreed unanimously.

Harvey's interview was a little more sober one and they focused on understanding the role of the casinos in the Professors life. At the end it was Devlin who asked they play back that part when first Miriam mentions the dangers she had anticipated. They rewound the tape and turned up the volume to hear what exactly she had said. Her voice was clear and they heard her say, **"Yes, I mean no, I don't know of any specific danger that he was in, but my fears had increased after all that cash came in from Las Vegas last year. Even Dennis felt uncomfortable with it and he had told me that he was going to stop his consultancy with them, he also told me vaguely that corruption comes into the system when insiders get greedy".**

This time they all caught the import of the words ". . . after all that cash came in from Las Vegas last year". They turned to Devlin who had been yesterday to question the CPA, a Jonathan Philer.

"The CPA told me that the Professor made up to a million dollars a year in the last ten years that by my reckoning is Ten million bucks, all of it is in the books and he says the Don used to be meticulous in paying his taxes. Where would the Cash come from then? The income that he got from the Casino companies, were all remitted to his banks here in California."

The implication was clear that there was more money involved than that the Professor got from the Casinos. Harvey having seen the huge hoard in the bank locker was sure the amount of cash was near 10 million or so. So a large amount of money that they could not reconcile with his declared income may have played a part in it. The difficulty lay in the fact that the killer had not benefited from the killing, he could not have that as his objective in committing the crime. The money in the locker was at best a spur that drove a man to kill another man.

Harvey then asked Devlin to give a complete brief of his questioning of the CPA.

"Philer has a small but stylish office near Kentfield Avenue, he has two or three people working for him, when I went in he became very nervous, very agitated . . ." At this point Megan interrupted him, "Sure he would be nervous, you march in there with your badge hanging out and announce that you there investigating the murder of his well healed client, wonder he didn't head straight to the can!" This was her way of telling Devlin, not to jump to a conclusion based on the reaction of that man.

Devlin continued, "I didn't mean to suggest that the man was nervous as he had something to hide, merely that the man was meek and not macho, anyway he put a pile of files in front of me and said that's the records of the man, and went on to say that his client was one of the more scrupulous ones in keeping his records straight".

No one in the room spoke there was an element here that had so far eluded them; if money was the key there might be something that could come from the CPA that could put them on a proper track.

Devlin had taken notes during his visit and he occasionally referred to them, "Philer told me that his client always came by his office with all the papers and bank statements and the withholding taxes and was not inclined to cut corners or seek to avoid tax on fee that he received for his talks abroad. Even if it was a token honorarium he reported it. If the invitation from overseas university came with a plane ticket he counted that as income too and then only deducted it. He also never charged off the expenses of his travels abroad if he used his own jet"

"Own Jet?" the question was a chorus from the others.

"Yeah! A Gulfstream 540" Devlin consulted his notes, "Seats eight, and flies .88 Mach" he looked up questioning them. What? Didn't they expect the professor to won a Jet?

A university professor owning a plane was not all that uncommon, but this was more like a corporate jet. He was not a Dot Com millionaire or an incorporated business that could afford or even desire of a plane that was pure indulgence. No response from anyone as they absorbed this detail

Devlin resumed from his notes, since they all seemed riveted by the mention of the Jet, he dwelt on the subject, "Keeps it at San Carlos Airport, where he is a member of a flying club, used to fly out on Friday and get back on Sunday morning most weekends, the flying club told me"

Harvey was happy that he had picked this rookie on his team; he was showing quite uncommon initiative.

Devlin came to the final part of his report, "The professor paid his taxes and had told the CPA that in case IRS called for an audit his papers were all in a locker, every bit of it, for safety. I told him that I would come back to collect the files from him and in the meantime to keep them safe, do you think I made a mistake in leaving it with him?"

Lieutenant Boskey assured him, "No mistake, in fact he would be guarding the papers with his life, those documents are his insurance in case any financial matters are involved in the murder, remember that if there is a link to the money in the murder, all those involved will get dragged into it as accessories to murder that could be well be an accountant."

So the team was now set on a firm course in their investigation, Follow the Money!

Chapter 8

IT'S A NUMBERS GAME

Harvey once again showed his skill in organizing the hunt, Megan was to connect with the Prosecutors office to get a formal warrant to take possession of the files from the Office of Mr. Jonathan Philer CPA, Devlin was to accompany her. Taggart was to organize an armoured truck to remove the cash in the bank locker and get to the Crime Lab where it could be counted and the amount reconciled with the financial records from the CPA office.

The team quickly dispersed on their task, Harvey stayed back to discuss something that had been bothering him and he thought Boskey would give him some insight.

Harvey started out by stating that he understood that the professor earned a lot of money by consulting for Casinos and that it was related to the business of the Casinos and that it was legitimate and except for the unaccounted cash found in the locker appeared to have paid the taxes on that.

The problem he said begins when he analyzed what Miriam had told him, she had said the Professor became fascinated by gambling in Macau and that he told her that he had found a way to beat the system and had a lot of winnings. So far, no problem. He later started to visit Las Vegas and according to Miriam consistently made money to attract the attention of the Casino security. That was followed by his offer to the casinos to help them. "What bothers me more is that I don't see the connection between his winning at the tables here in Vegas or in Macau and his work for the casinos."

Boskey began to get an idea where Harvey was leading his analysis. Even Boskey could not see the connection between winning at a table at any game with intuition, knowledge, fore knowledge or whatever and the subsequent work with the gaming machinery. In the light of the discovery of the cash the big question that loomed was, Did the professor after his engagement with Casino industry give up using his method to keep winning?.

Harvey said "Look at it this way, Miriam says that McPherson began to wager in Macau purely as a fun trip, obviously he wasn't carrying any device that would have helped him cheat. He began to win. He repeated that in Vegas. So it stands to reason that he had a method to win that had nothing to do with the machines, his offer to the casino was a diversion and a very lucrative one for him."

Boskey thought of the problem facing them, "The problem is that we know very little of gambling, much less of any means of cheating. We need someone to help us understand this. All I have heard of in cheating in Casinos is smart people counting cards or the kind in movies where they receive a feed from a mole, Devlin is the only who has talked to the people at the university, Let's ask him If any one talked about the work that Prof did for the Casinos".

Harvey called Devlin and asked him if he had spoken to anyone with a specific question on the Victims work for the casinos.

"Sure, I spoke to a Patrick Diggs, an associate professor in Statistics who said he had done some work for McPherson both in the university and also in Vegas!, here's his number"

Harvey couldn't wait to talk with the Patrick Diggs who could throw light on this very frustrating problem. Patrick on the phone appeared to be a cheerful individual and asked Harvey to come right over, not even asking why he wanted to meet.

Harvey sped towards the university. He hoped that this Patrick Diggs would throw some light on the how and what Professor did in particular on how he made his money. Consultancy fee a million dollars a year? Sure, if the casinos saved about a billion at the same time. There was also the question of his own belief that this service wasn't in any way illegal. There were far too many people involved. No corruption can stay hidden or work when it requires collusion of many. The gaming industry was tightly regulated, Nevada in particular was zealous in protecting its principal source of revenue, gambling comprised nearly all of its GDP. The state economy rested solely on the sales tax. One of the few states in the union not to have a personal income tax.

It had to be something else that brought in all that cash into play. At this point Harvey was convinced even before they began to work on the audit of the professors finances, they would find that the money was far too much than he had paid his taxes on. This view did not agree with what the CPA had said about the professor being meticulous in his tax filings and being an honest tax payer.

The professor was far too altruistic in not claiming legitimate deductions for his speaking engagement expenses. It did not agree with the profile of a meticulous man, there was no half way house to being meticulous, no way that he was on the way to achieving complete meticulousness in dealing with the IRS. Harvey thought sardonically that If he had a million coming in from some tax free source, what would a few dollars more of deduction matter.

Harvey entered the oval park at Stanford University and parked his car in the metered parking lot. He was tempted to slap the police sign on the dashboard, but decided against. Any one allowed to enter this place ought to be made to pay, he thought. He headed south as he had been told by Devlin and to look for Sloan Hall, the building for the mathematics department, he liked the well laid out environs with its' profusion of palms and envied the students such a place, he himself had been to a small community college, nothing like this beautiful campus, for his Bachelor degree in Criminal Management a prelude to joining the police force. He noted the mostly young looking students loitering around the grounds, not loitering, he told himself, and they were between classes enjoying the winter sun.

He found Dr. Patrick Diggs' office without difficulty, a lady staffer told him that Professor Diggs had stepped out to coffee and would be back soon, she invited him to wait in his chamber. On the door it said "Assistant Professor Diggs". The staff had referred to him as "Professor" elevating him in the esteem of the visitor who wouldn't know the difference.

Moments later Patrick Diggs bustled in hailing him, "How did you get here so fast, I bet you used your privilege of a siren, I myself wish for a siren to get through the traffic, you know get on the shoulder of the road . . ." he prattled on. Harvey noted his appearance; the guy could have been a student, maybe a slightly mature student. Except for the thinning hair he looked like the others that Harvey had seen on the way in. And he obviously liked to talk, no wonder that Devlin had taken to him and sent Harvey.

Patrick continued to talk, "I got myself a coffee do you want one, It's amazing that we are so addicted to coffee, it's absolutely American to be addicted to something or other, Soda, coffee, cocaine, pizzas, Chinese take away, We are even addicted to our political persuasion! Did you see the voting pattern in California the last 2 presidential elections? I can establish statistically that there has been no change, Democrats or Republican, any difference is like sampling error, see what I mean? I could go on" and he went on . . .

Harvey waited to get a word in edgewise, suddenly without pause the narration veered to the topic that had brought Harvey here. "You are because of the ghastly death of our math professor McPherson, nice chap, and you want to know if anyone at the university had any reason to go get a gun and shoot him?, No I don't think so, he was a nice guy and we in the pure sciences don't develop pure hatred, What do you think, a student gets poor grades goes and offs the teacher?, No not here, the fact that he is a student here means we wouldn't have to flunk him, unless he is a nut" he chortled.

Incredibly the torrent of words stopped, giving Harvey his chance to take control of the enquiry, "Actually I was interested in knowing more about your collaboration with the professor in his work for the casinos"

"It was nice, in fact very nice of him to ask me and paid well too, I got myself a new BMW, my old car was falling apart, you don't get that kind of money out here. Maybe if you get tenure and a grant but for me that's a long way off. Like I said it was nice, but you said Collaboration, there wasn't any collaboration; he just took me along to test some algorithms. Let me tell you it was all first class we flew down in his Jet and we get into this fabulous hotel and the Casino treated him like royalty I myself was a minor royal for those few days last year before the spring quarter."

No dearth of details there, Harvey stuck to his purpose stubbornly, "What algorithms?"

"Oh! Algorithms, I see that you want to know EXACTLY what Professor McPherson did for the casinos, gambling and all that, it has a fatal fascination you know, it's like any other addiction like I said before, I can tell you all about it, do you have time? It can take some time, can I get that coffee for you so we can talk"

Harvey had both the time and the inclination, he nodded. Asst. Professor Patrick Diggs got up to get that addictive coffee and then turned around and said, "It's all in the numbers, you know?"

Chapter 9

THE LINKS OF A CHAIN

Megan & Devlin made their way to the District Attorney's office. As they entered Megan spotted Lisa Raymond, one of the hundred or so of the DA's assistants. Megan had only a nodding acquaintance with Lisa but they greeted each other familiarly, after all they were sisters in public service. Lisa had joined the DA's office only a month ago from a stint in the City Attorneys' office. A short internship at the City Attorney's had turned into a two year sentence, before finding the position in the DA's office she spent her most enjoyable time when she was assigned the Permits Section. Those she displaced were not pleased, one long term occupier of Permits was openly resentful and she could not understand why. Very soon she got the idea, Permits is the place where visitors were all supplicants, citizens came in timidly fearing failure to get past the regulations of the mighty San Mateo county, a hint of corruption was all it took for Lisa to bolt for safer pastures. In fact the city attorney had got wind of the goings on and had posted her before the stink spread beyond the four walls of the office.

In her new job, Lisa Raymond did not have an easier time, as a newbie she was required to go before all courts, before a Trial date was set, the defense moved a number of pre-trial motions and that included motions for continuance. The DA's office was required to be present, Lisa was the DA's office, continuance granted in court and she rushed to the next court hall. She had become in four weeks very familiar with the court halls of the Southern Branch of the Superior Court of California, San Mateo.

They told her what they wanted and she had a word with her immediate superior and agreed to fill up the Search & Seizure warrant request form, she filled in the details and Devlin gave the details of the deceased and the CPA's address at which they wanted to execute the warrant. Having done that they went in to the Hall of Justice, they would have to find a judge in his chambers. Lisa found that a Judge, The Hon Luke Brewster was in his chamber. Lisa told them he was known to the legal fraternity as Judge Brewer especially after lunch. They entered his chamber at his command and were met by his baleful glance, he did not hide a belch, and the Hon Brewer had finished a late and leisurely lunch. He silently took the form and Lisa began to nervously explain that it was a matter of urgency (why they just couldn't wait till after his siesta) and said it was a case of murder.

"Who is the deceased?" he asked, Lisa hurriedly said "Professor Dennis McPherson, he was a Professor at Stanford".

The last part was a big mistake, an unnecessary detail, The Judge roughly four decades ago had been to the university and held his Alma Mater in high regard, and now this chit of a girl two years out of law school wants to seize financial records that too of Professor there.

"Why do you want his financial records, is he being investigated for Tax evasion?"

"NO, Your honor, just that it might be linked to his homicide!"

Grudgingly he took up the request form again and motioned to Megan "you have signed this? You should not have signed this in both places, this here is for you to sign in my presence, he indicated the place, doesn't matter, I will take it is you who have signed this, I think you have an honest face!"

Megan sincerely hoped that the judge couldn't see her honest face, the occasion called for her most dishonest face. Devlin had become alarmed, having lately become aware of her reputation for wisecracks he held his breath.

Megan though, restrained herself admirably in spite of a strong urge and they emerged triumphant from the judge's chamber.

Outside Megan turned to Lisa, "I forgot to thank the Judge, you think I should send him a bottle of brew?"

Lisa's laughter echoed around the hallowed hall of Justice.

Taggart in the meanwhile approached his task with confidence, easy as pie, he called the first armored car company and wanted to hire one to transport some valuables within the city limits, the armored car guy said "Sure, come on over we need to do some paperwork before we start"

Zack, the armored car company guy had a villainous face, perfect for launching a hundred bad guy roles. Casting directors would have no difficulty in casting him. He had such raw natural talent—his face. Taggart was however reassured by the certificates, licenses & permits hanging on the walls of his office. Zack the villain, pulled a long form and demanded, "Where to where"

"In the city itself, a couple of miles at most"

"Distance doesn't matter, we charge by the hour but there is a minimum" He mentioned the minimum.

Taggart was jolted by the amount, he didn't show that he was staggered, he now represented the exalted office of the county sheriff and had to uphold the dignity of that high office and thanked almighty that this guy didn't talk percentages and didn't know the amount involved.

He nodded mutely.

Having before him a prospective customer, Zack's face softened, a little, he could now play the role of a reformed felon saved by the kindness of a benevolent judge.

More answers were needed to fill in the forms. "What's the value of the merchandise?"

"Around ten million dollars" No reaction there, Villains are very hard to impress.

"Name of your insurance carrier and amount insured"

Taggart was puzzled, what insurance?, he had life insurance, group insurance, accident insurance, car insurance, health insurance, home insurance . . . "mine?"

"Yeah, it's your merchandise isn't it?"

Taggart was about to say that the merchandise belonged to a dead guy, but decided against sharing it when this guy had no need to know. Need to know basis was standard in spy movies.

"No, it is not mine, it's in a bank and I have to take it for safe custody to the sheriff's office, it's not any merchandise it's cash and I am a cop" There he said it, it's now official business.

"You want take cash, that's not yours, that's in a bank and take it in an armored truck to the Sheriff?" His tone suggesting, no, implying, that no Sheriff worth his salt would agree to a plan to knock off a bank and then have it brought to his office in an armored truck to share the loot.

Zack got back to business, "Does the sheriff have insurance?" Then showing patience "for transporting Cash, insurance with a standard insurance company?"

Taggart had an answer to that, why would the sheriff have insurance to carry cash, he could call a couple of cruisers to follow him. "No"

"If the sheriff doesn't have insurance we cannot transport cash for him"

"Don't you have insurance? And you carry cash around for banks?"

"Sure we do that's our business, but we have insurance and they have insurance, because we have insurance we carry the cash for them, they give us the cash because they the insurance to transport it, Transit Insurance!"

It was clear to Taggart that he was not going to get anywhere with this guy and went in search of a less regulation bound cash carrier. Two other companies reported similar inability. Taggart then decided that the time had come for direct action. Having made his decision, he hired a moving company van along with two helpers. Asking them to stop at a packaging company store, he bought a few corrugated cartons two feet by one and half and threw the collapsed cartons into the back of the van. He then asked to drive to the bank telling them to park at the side door, a door clearly marked employees only. No stopping at any time. The help crew looked fearfully at the CC TV cameras at the front, the back, over the door. He told them to wait; he would call them when he was ready. He strode to the front of the bank and having stuffed the cartons with the cash from the locker, stepped out of the side door and beckoned them inside. Quaking in their shoes that they had been inveigled into participating in a bank heist they carried the cartons and took off in double quick time. Taggart came into the Crime Lab and happily handed the document guy the cartons and got him sign an acknowledgement for cash received being the entire contents of bank locker as certified by a bank manager.

The triumphant duo of Megan and Devlin marched into the office of Jonathan Philer CPA, who seemed to have anticipated their arrival and had placed all the files pertaining to his now dead client in a pile and pointed it to them as they arrived. Next he handed them an envelope full of CD's and explained that they were the backup files of his client year wise. It seems that Philer was also maintaining the accounts of his client on the computer. Devlin asked him, "How are we going to access those files, is there a password?"

"The password is Prof Title 26" he said and Devlin thought, that figures, the password is a direct reference to the professors Federal Taxes record. Philer told them the computer accounting software versions had changed over the years and they would need both the older version and the new one.

Then Philer produced an itemized list of documents contained in the files, the list was 28 pages long, Megan and Devlin heaved a sigh of relief. It was what they wanted; the seizure warrant had a box for entering the details of seized materials and would have taken a day for them to fill. Now all they had to do was enter "As per Annexed list". They thanked the surprised accountant profusely.

They left hurriedly with the precious records one that could establish the mystery, Money whence it came and why it led to murder in the first degree. On reaching the Crime Lab they made their way to the Financial Forensics section. Devlin spotted the Document Man who had been at the scene of the crime the first day of investigation and noting the name badge on his lab coat greeted him by name. "Hey Larsen, we got something for you".

Megan idly wondered why a Financial Forensics man had to wear a lab coat, supposing that you work in a place called a lab, ergo! You wore a lab coat.

The document man was pleased that the cop remembered his name and delighted to take charge of the new material from them. He was especially pleased with the backup files in the computer accounting package used by the CPA. Soon he was busy collating the information as a spread sheet for a ten year period. Megan & Devlin waited patiently. Larsen finally finished his computation and put it up on the big screen. It was a facsimile of a Federal Tax return 1040, which they had seen a lot of time and used it themselves. But the significance of the numbers was not clear to them.

Larsen excitedly pointed out the details, "This here is his income from the University, close to a million dollars over the period of ten years, this is his other income . . . ." and he stopped abruptly, something about the massive amount there causing his jaw to drop, he began scrolling down to check on the details. Having satisfied himself about the accuracy, he returned to his explanation.

"See this line in the Fed Tax Form, see this line 21, that's his Other Income and it's close to ten million dollars over these ten years and most of it is from gambling!" the last bit said in awe of the prowess of the player.

"You sure?" a surprised chorus from Megan and Devlin.

"Yeah, I checked, see here are the W 2 G's for the latest year, I am sure they are all there for the earlier years also. That's the withholding tax forms issued by the casinos."

"Do casinos withhold federal taxes on winnings?" Devlin wanted to know, in the tone of one lamenting 'nothing is sacrosanct in taxes'.

"No, they don't normally withhold all winnings, only if it's large and may do if they are asked by the winner, and in any case if the winnings are large it makes sense to ask them to withhold, it saves a lot of hassles later and you don't have to wait till January for them to send this form to you" Larsen said holding up a small form.

"What if I lose money at the tables?" Devlin was still riled at the avarice of the Federal Government, virtually grabbing money that had been won from a casual fling at gambling.

"The Tax code is fair, it allows you to write off losses too, but only to the extent of your winnings in that same year, but if you have lost more than you have won, then that loss is what you lose, am I making sense here; you understand what I am saying?" Larsen said trying to explain a small part of the Internal revenue code that someone had estimated would fill up 7500 pages IF they could fit in 60 lines to a page.

Megan chipped in "Sure I understand, the feds don't take a loss from nobody!"

Megan then zeroed in on the question of the cash found in the locker, "How much cash did he have?" The question was wrongly worded as she was soon to discover.

"Let's see" Larsen turned back to the computer "Cash and Cash Equivalent in his accounts show a sum of nearly 5 million, that is comprised of cash, stocks & shares, bonds, Insurance funds, Pension funds, annuities, term deposits . . . ."

The cops didn't let him finish "Could he have put aside a cash hoard of 10 million in a locker?"

"No, the amount of loose cash and I use the term loosely would be around half a mil to a mil . . ."

They had the answer now, the professor was no tax cheat on his gambling winnings, and he had paid taxes on them.

The question, whence did the cash come from? That remained a mystery.

At the University, Harvey was being an attentive listener to Assistant Professor Patrick Diggs. Who had set about the task of informing the uninformed? He reveled in the role of the teacher chosen to bring esoteric knowledge to a homicide investigation. Over cups of addictive coffee, he began simplifying the response to his new disciple.

"Algorithms are simply put a set of instructions to arrive at an outcome in finite number of steps. Algorithms are relatively new or I should say a product of 20th Century advances in computing, you want computer to compute something for you, you gave the instructions as a series of steps that it had to do. Simply put they are commands set out in a particular order. Am I being clear" he asked his target audience much like in a class room.

"Now ask yourself, what is gambling? It is the chance that a particular event will occur, if your wager is on the correct number or card you win. The risk reward equation in gambling is affected randomly. The best example is the slot machine, you put in a coin, pull the handle and a series of number come up, if those numbers match the winning combo, you win if it doesn't you lose. The sequence of numbers or symbols coming up in a slot machine is purely random." Thus far Harvey had no problem following the exposition.

"In computer controlled gaming machines the program generates the random event, but it cannot be so random that the winning combination is truly random, the gambler will walk away if he sees no wins in a few attempts, so they program the machine to bring up the winning numbers every once in a while. The Gaming laws also make it mandatory to reward the players with 75% of the betting the wager. It's not that every gambler wins 75% of his wagers back but over a period of time on an average a single machine should be so designed that it pays out 75%, that's where the Algorithm plays a part. Prof McPherson found a way to ensure that the casinos operate on the right side of law and pay out the 75% and not more than that, Any Questions?"

Finding his student nodding vigorously Patrick continued, "A casino has many types of games and of course, they cannot actually manipulate some games like Blackjack, though Blackjack has an inbuilt bias for the Dealer, the other players have to beat the dealer to win. Some small wager machines are like the slot machines, also called Fruit machines, they are the old favorites. They are not fixed in any way, it is only in Semi-Automated and fully Automated Machines that some fixing can be done and it has to be done such that the gaming commission does not know about it, which I can tell you is very difficult, they are good and pull the license of any casino that is found to have manipulated the machines. They are serious about it. So whatever the Professor did for the Casinos were for a few types of machines. If he has done it all these years then it goes to show that it was not illegal and certified by an accredited testing laboratory".

"The catch you see is to have a program that pays near normal yet has a safety valve that pays out for a machine is at or around the 75% pay-out ratio. The casinos report the winnings and the number of plays, number of people at a particular table are all filed with the commission. Since they get the data from all licensed casinos they can compare the data and catch any unusual figures from a casino and even a particular game machine"

Harvey focused his question on his recollection of the Professor's wife Miriam telling him that her husband had something about understanding the paradox. "Is there is a paradox in the way a Gaming machine works?" that's the best he could do to put into words his impression that the professor may have discovered some such formula that made him a unique expert.

"No, No paradox, not in the way the machine works, has worked, nor in the results of the casinos has shown any paradox" Patrick was firm. Harvey was silent he had come to a dead end.

Patrick felt sorry that he could not help this detective in some way, he could sense the disappointment. So in an attempt to cheer him up he added "You know the professor was a diehard fan of gambling, that's a bit strange when you think about it, he more than anyone knew that in the long run the gambler would lose, the odds are in favor of the house. There is even a paradox called the Gambler's Paradox, there you have it! The great Paradox, the man who knew it all and should not have gambled at all, was nothing but a gambler".

Harvey rose from his seat feeling lightheaded, something that Patrick had said about addiction and his last statement that Professor was a gambler came together in a flash, and the Professor was a gambling addict!"

Harvey had one more question, "Could the professor have manipulated the gaming machines in such a way, the he and he alone could win at will?"

It was a categorical shake of the head of Patrick "Impossible, I am sure that he won and lost as much as any other player, but the man to tell about how much he won and how much he lost would be Pfeiffer of Topkapi Casino, the professor played there most all the time, the other casinos he only played when the gaming machines were on field trial as ordered by the Gaming Commission".

Harvey thanked the Assistant Professor Patrick for his most helpful assistance in the matter and prepared to leave, Patrick was gratified by the grace of this detective who seemed so intent on catching the killer. So helpfully he suggested "You should meet Dr. Murphy as well, he and Dennis used to be together all the time and both shared interest in Probability, but be prepared for a less than warm welcome, I should say a very gruff welcome if at all, he has not been himself lately, flies off the handle quite easily, the students have been steering clear of him they tell me".

Harvey had a question, "Was he this way before Dr. McPherson's murder?"

"Oh! I am sorry, I said lately, such an imprecise expression, he has been out of sorts, and not just after the loss of his friend, but even before, I would say since the start of the Fall Quarter."

This did not tell Harvey anything, so okay a professor had turned nutty, flipped a switch, it could be anything, marital problems, money problem, hell he could even be like the sergeant at Narcotics who suddenly became abusive towards the whole force and had to be sent for counseling which didn't help, eventually it was found that the poor guy had been living with the bacteria *Helicobacter pylori* in his stomach acids and that had tormented the living daylights out of him. Having decided to come back to meet with the irascible Don, he bade goodbye and started back to HQ.

On the way his cell phone rang with Megan calling with the news of their discovery of the dead professors financial situation, even before she could start giving the details of the findings, Harvey interjected, "I bet there is nothing in there in his financial records about his gambling!" He rashly surmised that a gambling addict would not have left records that could reach the IRS even if privacy was guaranteed by laws.

"WRONG" boomed Megan's voice from the tiny cell phone. She liked things crystal clear, life's uncertainties upset her, so she made clear crisply that her partner had read the tea leaves wrong! Harvey almost missed the exit towards HQ.

She went to explain that the professor through the years had meticulously reported his gambling income and the income from the consulting work for the casinos as well as his lecture fee and had paid his taxes. The remittances from the casinos comprised mostly his winnings as well as the consulting fee, presumably done as a favor to him instead of having to carry cash back home.

Harvey turned into the parking lot of the office and did not enter the building and sat in the car and thought. Cash is king they say; here in this case, Cash was a clue. Where did it lead? Who did it point to? No one. He had presumed McPherson as a gambler and a cheat. Gambler true but cheat NO!

So what did the cash hoard in the second bank locker represent? If not from gambling where did it come from?

Then another thought struck him, Patrick had said that the Professor won and lost as much as any other player. In which case his winnings over the ten year period was way too enormous! Gambling winnings and losses accrued over time, presumably while winning he had also lost some money. Why presumably almost certainly during this period he would have lost if not an equal amount, a fairly large sum! If he had lost half what he had declared as his income the amount would total 15 million dollars? He grabbed the phone and called Megan. Did he also declare his losses, claim it as a deduction as a matter of course?

Megan answered in the negative. So his reckoning was correct, the amount involved was at a minimum of 15 million dollars. How did the casinos not notice his regular jackpots? His wagers were definitely not penny ante, they were obviously high stakes. Did he play the high end tables with a minimum wager of say a thousand dollars? High roller?

A high roller was most welcome at the casinos; he was welcome so long as he left something behind on the table. A high roller such as the one who breaks the bank regularly wouldn't be welcomed with complimentary suites and free drinks. They would watch him and catch him!

The security at the casinos in Las Vegas had some very unusual protection, they could detain a person on suspicion, no illegal arrest or detention charges could be brought against them. Let alone criminal liability, the casino had no civil liability in such cases.

On the contrary he was treated as Royalty; even Patrick Diggs did not mind the Minor Royal status conferred on him.

He was certain in his mind that the professor had beaten all odds in accumulating the money and somehow escaped the attention of the IRS. A Clever man, who had somehow snapped a vital link in a chain that would have tied him to the cash.

Chapter 10

THE QUEST FOR THE CONNECTION

Harvey went up to the office to find the team waiting for him; Megan alone retained the optimism of cracking the case. Taggart seemed eager to set off on any task given him; Devlin had a distracted look, as if he was puzzled at the turn of events. They compared notes on the day's events, Megan said finding that the Professor had declared his gambling wins in his taxes somehow brought relief to her; she had been quite disquieted by suspicion that a university Don would be a Tax cheat.

They all had one common object to focus attention on, the cash hoard in the bank. The answer to that question seemed of the utmost importance. Having ruled out illegal gambling receipts or tax evasion they had to look for a source of that money. Who had that kind of money? Obviously the involvement of Casinos in the equation was a pointer.

Harvey told them now the two persons to focus were Dr. Murphy who might know dead professor and a certain Mr. Pfeiffer of Topkapi casino. The other members involved, Harvey explained, "Miriam, the wife of the deceased, David the son, and Elle the family friend were at this moment not 'Persons of Interest'". The others noted his choice of words to term Elle as a friend of the family than as a part time maid. Hardened Cops too have delicate feelings.

The description of someone as 'Person of Interest' gave a lot of leeway to investigators, they could be called in for questioning, and their premises could be searched— albeit with a warrant. The investigator has a justifiable reason to keep such a person in close personal contact. This close and personal contact may sometime engender a warm and fuzzy feeling.

Even before they had decided on splitting the duties for the next day, Harvey was on the phone asking Elle If they could meet for dinner, hearing her OK, he turned to them with a happy face. Megan was both happy and afraid for him; she knew Susan and feared that were she to know that Harvey had been to dinner with a young woman, very likely she would complain to the chief, that her husband was involved in the course of his duties with a person likely to harm her married life. The chief would not be able to ignore the complaint, terming it as a domestic or personal issue, the matter involved a potential suspect and a definite witness, he would have to act and remove Harvey from the investigation.

Harvey himself seemed unconcerned and they decided that next morning Harvey and Megan would go to Las Vegas for an interview with Mr. Pfeiffer. While Devlin would revisit Dr. Murphy at the University, but this time accompanied by Taggart. Dr. Murphy might try and browbeat a fresh faced rookie cop but not a tough street wise cop like Taggart.

Harvey hurried out of the office and headed to Elle's house in Friendly Acres not far from his office, Elle invited him in to meet her two young sons, and they greeted him with smiles and said they wanted to go to Woodside High when they grew up. Elle seemed confident they would behave even when she left them alone.

Harvey had called and booked a table at Desmond's, a romantic restaurant if ever there was one in Redwood City. Only when they were in the car did Elle ask him where they were headed.

"Desmond's" said and didn't add that he wanted a private and intimate dinner. He liked Desmond's, a fine restaurant renowned for its wines and food. He liked the owner better, Desmond was a legend in the restaurant business, and it would seem everyone knew Desmond or he knew everyone. He seemed to remember every customer and what they liked to eat.

In fact, for Harvey, Desmond's had become a refuge, whenever he returned from work and the situation threatened to become acrimonious, he suggested to Susan that they go to Desmond's. It would improve her mood, it would get much better after they entered Desmond's, where the host greeted them warmly and paid special attention to Susan.

Elle saw the restaurant for the first time, Ivy covered two storey structure, and it looked like an expensive place even from the outside. Turning the corner, they parked behind the restaurant and walked to the front, Elle casually reached and held his hand as they entered. Desmond was in attendance, ever the discreet diplomat he did not mention Susan but turned his full attention to Elle, Harvey was ignored, forgotten for the moment as he lavished his charm on his beautiful guest Elle.

Harvey could see that Elle enjoyed the attention, considered asking for a private dining room, Desmond's was a place famous for its private dining room, and it was where million dollars deals were struck by the Silicon Valley entrepreneurs. But instead asked to be seated near the bar, the restaurant did not fit the image of a romantic spot, it was brightly lit and the tables were large with seating for large groups, a few tables were arranged in the corners for twosomes.

They were at ease with each other and conversed easily. Harvey having been partner with Megan had picked up humor and began regaling Elle with the funny situations in the serious cop business. As they talked and relaxed the ever present distraction of their life at present, the murder and its aftermath, was difficult to avoid, it was this 'white noise' that made Elle ask how the investigation was going.

Harvey began casually, "The investigation is progressing, we have a couple of leads." it was as if he was answering at a press conference and suddenly he sprang it on her, "Did you know your Dennis has stashed away ten million cash in a bank locker . . ." he stopped himself from uttering the challenge, I bet you didn't know about it!.

Elle reacted with surprise and shock, surprised by the implication that her benefactor was involved in criminal activity and the shock of seeing the man sitting in front of her who moments ago seemed to have the light of love in his eyes regard her as complicit in a criminal enterprise.

Even as the words passed his lips Harvey had felt the regret of such thoughtless words and felt deeply that he had virtually stabbed her with his gestapo tactics. He quickly moved to make amends and words poured from him in torrent to contain the damage that he had caused. He spoke non-stop till he could see that she appeared mollified with his explanation that he himself was surprised.

He decided then and there, impulsively, to share the details of what he and the team had uncovered during the investigation. She would definitely help, he was certain; in any way that she could, to help in the hunt for the man who had killed her mentor and savior.

Sitting across the table would not do, he moved to her side and asked for a writing pad and scribbled down the facts as they had unearthed. He finally underlined too words, Gambling Income and Cash Stash.

Elle turned to him to ask, "Gambling income? You mean what the casinos paid him?"

Harvey shook his head, "No he made a lot of money gambling!" he said this in a flat voice, no inflexions to imply anything but a statement of bare facts.

"How do you know?" Elle was still puzzled.

"It's there in his tax returns, year after year" leaving her in no doubt that it was indeed a fact.

Elle desperately tried to recall seeing a line for Gambling income in her federal tax returns, it was all there isn't it, the instructions that said, enter here, and do not enter here. And then another thought, "If he had gambling income in Las Vegas, that's Nevada and Nevada has no income tax, right?"

Harvey explained that it was Federal Tax and that there was even a withholding tax provision. Elle gave up on understanding of the income tax code; it was enough for her know that Dennis had indeed made money by gambling and that he had honestly paid up his taxes on it.

Harvey then turned to the other item in his list, the Cash Stash; this he explained was the most mysterious of the facts unearthed. Where did the money come in? And why did Dennis put it into his bank locker? And why he did not, if it was legitimate, declare it in his returns? The answer to any of those questions could very well lead them to solve the murder mystery.

He began to tell her what he had surmised so far as to the cash found in the locker. It was definitely linked somehow to his link with the casinos, if one were to look for a large enough source of such money, obviously the Professor was not knocking off banks, so the casino connection was present.

So one connection could be made, two dots connected, at one end of the connection was the Professor at the other end was the casinos, but whom in the casinos?

Then he set out his other disquiet, the apparent improbability that the gambling wins of the professor came about in the normal course of a play. He explained with some simple calculations.

"See here, Dennis or Den as you call him, made a million dollars a year for ten years, a million, you understand, each year, maybe there are others in that bracket of players who clear that kind of money, I don't know tomorrow I shall check in Vegas they may be able to tell me. But we know from his habits that he used to fly his jet to Vegas on Fridays and return on Sunday, so for at least 50 days he had a chance to play at the tables, for net a million dollars, he would have to average 20 grand at every visit to Vegas. That's hard to believe, that's a rate that defies the odds in games of chance."

He paused letting Elle absorb the import of his words, "He seemed to have done the impossible! Every year for ten years! According to the professor at the university I spoke to today, even the professor won and lost as much as any player, that's his take."

"So If he has won that much and assuming that he had a way to do it, how much were his losses, If not an equal amount, it must have been in some proportion to his winning, by my reckoning that could be a half a million a year. Now where did that money he lost come from?"

Elle understood what Harvey was trying to convey to her, that the professor's plays were so very large as net him a clear win of a twenty thousand dollar every time that he played. Even if that was a rough average, it boggled the mind.

The Harvey came to the unanswered question in his mind as to the role played by the casinos themselves in this, "How? I am asking myself did the Casinos let this happen, it's not a casual first time lucky winner walking away with a twenty grand cash, here a well-known figure walked in every single weekend and cleared them of a sum net of losses, they would have watched him as they do every customer that walks in the door, a friend has told me that there are more CC TV Cameras in Las Vegas than residents! He could not have escaped attention of the cameras that record every single move of the players."

"So, answer me this riddle, why would security watching him beat the casino not stop him?, they are rough with anyone they suspect of cheating, they have some sort of immunity even in detaining a person, but if they actually catch a cheat he is in for a bad time, it seems recently some US Supreme Court ruling has put a crimp in their style from claims of civil damages, but not if a Gaming Board agent is around, And Gaming Board agents generally side with the casinos security otherwise they would not be enforcing any law at all, so if they catch a cheat with evidence, that guy is not going to sue for damages he would be licking his wounds in state prison."

Harvey fell silent, he had told her all of his doubts and laid out for her consideration, Elle was impressed by the intensity that he put into the case, and there was no hesitation on her part that his analysis was indeed plausible.

Desmond had been watching them having an animated discussion and stayed away but now he decided to enter their private space, he couldn't accept that Harvey and that beautiful woman would come into his restaurant and not enjoy the food at all.

Very soon their table was laden with wine and food, all of it put there by Desmond of his own choice without demur from his guests. They finally walked out into the night with Elle clutching Harvey's arm in the chill air. They parted as comfortably as old friends and sans any awkward goodbyes. They planned to see each other at the Inquest into the death of Prof McPherson to be held by the Coroner in two days' time.

Chapter 11

THE PLAYER IN THE GAME

In the morning Harvey and Megan made their way separately to San Francisco airport and met as agreed at the American Airline counter, the aircraft was only half full, apparently flying to sin city this early did not appeal to the holiday crowd. Harvey settled in his seat in the economy class, he suspected that the office had hunted down the cheapest fare flights out to Las Vegas for them, he opened the newspaper that he found in the seat pouch and turned to international news, the news was routine and yet another suicide bomber had scored a grizzly toll in Iraq, no US casualties. Then two reports on Air Travel, the first was a protest by the US representative to the U.N. Complaining that UN Staff almost exclusively travelled by Club Class and thus drained its coffers. The second from India, where a minister, forced to downgrade to Economy termed it as 'Cattle Class' which seemed to have touched off an uproar in that country. Cattle equal cows and scrawny cows are Holy in that ancient land. The scrawny cow bit had been told by a friend who had been on trip there 'scrawny cows squat on the road and everyone goes around them', so scrawny urban cows with the right of way!

He turned to his economy class fellow traveler to share this bit of international news, to find that she was reading a large hardbound book, curiosity bitten he asked "What are you reading?" "History of the Geography of America" an involuntary "Whaaat?" escaped his lips. She laughed heartily causing the flight attendant near them to look up fearfully. "Did you know that we did not know California was here . . . ." her finger pointing to the floor of the plane ". . . . till the start of the nineteen century?"

"Who did not know California was here?" asked Harvey, offended that Megan had freely included him in the universe of the ignorant.

"The cartographers, you know the map makers? The survey people? The maps of those times never showed California as we know it!"

Harvey retreated in the face of 'in your face knowledge' and waited for the flight to land at Las Vegas.

They exited the terminal building at McCarran Airport and waiting for them was Captain Robert Flake, Harvey was surprised and pleased, a professional courtesy he hadn't expected. They got into his car and headed towards the Metropolitan Police Department building, on the way, Captain Flake said that on receiving Harvey's

call he had told his boss, D/C Donna Waller the head
of the Investigative Services Division, who in turn had
informed her superior Assistant Sheriff Robbins. They
seemed extremely interested in any connection between
the death of a professor in San Carlos and the Las Vegas
Casino Industry.

So they headed straight to the swank new building
of the Metropolitan Police and were truly awed at
the ultra-modern feel of the building, they passed
a situation room which had a wall display that was
currently tracking a traffic incident and the Patrol
response to it, the cars converging to the scene, a
separate corner of the screen was showing the live feed
from the traffic cam at the scene. The visitors who were
from the Silicon Valley celebrated as the tech center of
the world were humbled. "Our Mayor should see this"
whispered Megan.

They were courteously received by the Assistant Sheriff
and D/C Waller. After the preliminaries Harvey stood
up and made a crisp presentation, he was precise
and didn't have to refer any notes. He told them
of the Victims financial affairs and the conclusion
that he was deeply connected to the casinos in Las
Vegas for a number of years, the fact that a large sum
of unaccounted money was found in a bank locker.
All of which merited investigation into the possible
involvement of someone within the casino industry.

Donna Waller spoke next, "I and my division offer you
full and complete cooperation in your investigation,
there will be no issues of turf or territorial assertion, we

in the Sheriff's office are extremely concerned about the possibility that what has happened in San Mateo County has its origin here. You can ask and receive any assistance that you and your partner here Megan wants, Capt. Robert Flake will be your point man, at this time we have no information that any crime has occurred in this jurisdiction so our role is that of a local agency extending unreserved help. You may carry out any investigation of any nature, but for your safety I suggest that you always take the help and advice of Captain Flake. Please do not attempt to venture by yourself if the situation appears to be risky, I don't doubt your competence to handle such situation by yourself, but any unforeseen eventuality will reflect on our law enforcement. Any findings of your please feel free to bring it to us first, we assure that there will be no leaks that would affect your investigation, the Assistant Sheriff joins me to vouch for that. We wish to handle this with utmost discretion keeping in mind the effect of any adverse disclosure on the casino industry that would have a bearing on the economy of the state."

It was a polished, practiced speech and you couldn't doubt the competence of the person delivering that. Donna then added "For your stay we arranged a hotel nearby here that is safe which we regularly use for our guests" and then she laughed "not the state guests we put behind bars!"

Harvey wasn't going to refuse the help and promise of cooperation offered by the Metropolitan police in a city he wasn't familiar with. It would also the lift the load on them and to call upon resources was something that they could not imagine in their own city.

Their hotel turned out to be a luxurious one; obviously the County Clarke wasn't hurting from budget woes to be able to offer such hospitality to its guests.

Now the three of them Harvey, Megan and Flake sat down to draw up the first point of contact with the casinos. Pfeiffer of Topkapi Casino was first on the list, in fact the only one that Harvey had with him, and he had vague plans of meeting some people from the Gaming Board and the manufacturers.

The others targets could wait, Harvey called Pfeiffer and asked if they could meet in connection with the death of McPherson. Pfeiffer didn't show the least surprise, the murder had made the national news and had disappeared into the inside pages of the newspapers after just two days. The only media following the case was the local TV and News at Redwood City. He didn't respond with the obvious question, "What you want to talk to me about?"

To give the impression that the visit was purely from the San Mateo County in California and no local police was involved it was decided that Flake would remain in the lobby. As they approached Topkapi Casino, Flake provided a little background on the hotel itself, "It's one of the older ones, not very popular and not like the others which have regular updates and changes to keep fresh, and you can say the place is a little rundown"

As they turned a corner, Flake pointed out a tower on his left as the Topkapi Tower & Casino, Megan was disappointed, and "It doesn't look very impressive".

Flake agreed, "It was originally planned to be a large tower some 30 stories high, but they had problems with the site and had to scale it down to 15, the plans never recovered after that change, you know in this town there are a lot of strange beliefs and locals have always believed that the place is jinxed!"

"What happened with the original plan? They run out of money?" asked Harvey.

"It's the site that was the problem, the consultant had given a report that the ground was suitable for the Tower planned but added that there would be subsidence, you know the ground settling because of the weight of the building, well the building sank alright and the work had to stop because the city got involved and ordered the construction to stop. There were a lot of law suits, the promoters sued the consultant, the contractor sued the consultant, the consultant counter sued the structural guys and so on the work was held up for more than 2 years and the original promoters then sold the building in 'as is where is conditions' and got out of it."

"Even then the casino would not have got off the ground if not for Bruce Trent, the new owner who made a lot of noise in the media that red tape was killing the industry and we just couldn't compete with the threat from far and near, far being Macau and near being Atlantic City in New Jersey."

Harvey wanted to know about Bruce Trent, "Does he live here in Vegas?"

"Yes!, He is one of the most flamboyant characters in the City, He is said to be savvy, smart and he has kept the casino going on well over 10 years now. He keeps pulling tourists into the joint by any means, he employed these touts who would catch people just getting off the bus and steer them straight to Topkapi, and he had the tour operator's drive right up to the casino as the first stop in Las Vegas. The city slapped a number of notices on him for irregular employment, other employment codes but pays the fine and still turns a decent profit from it, ironically his latest is a venture to have a Casino in Macau, which he had said was the greatest threat to Las Vegas!.

Harvey and Megan walked through the lobby, which to their eyes, unaccustomed to the glitz and glamour of Las Vegas, appeared just fine and not run down as Flake had told them. They entered Pfeiffer's office on an upper floor, it was large and they had to walk the length of the room to reach his desk behind which he waited for them. Ever since Mussolini, everyone in need of boost to self-esteem had adopted this tactic of a long room and a high desk so as to look down upon their visitor. Harvey did not miss the psychology and its pointer to this man, a vital focus in their investigation.

As they made their way to the desk, Harvey checked the man and his manner. He appeared physically fit and had shaved his head. His clothes were undoubtedly high end. His face betrayed no emotion, that was it, No welcome, No hostility either, Neutral like a seasoned Poker player.

"Prof McPherson was a consultant to us for a long time, I would say since the day we opened our doors, he used his expertise in advising us in maintaining the winning edge, it's a thin edge, the profit margin I mean. A casino is a gambler on the other side of the table. The fact is that we are not in the top league, we don't have high roller tables, except two, all others are in the small minimum range. You can say we are in the nickel and dime business range of the casinos"

Harvey asked him, "You mean to say the players never can make big money here?" displaying the typical ignorance of out of towners.

"No, I don't mean that, Oh! They can clear a jackpot like in any other joint, what I meant was that here a player can start with a table minimum of 5 dollars. In fact it gives them that much more fun, as they can play longer instead of losing everything in one shot, we keep our visitors far longer that way"

Pfeiffer appeared to relax, these cops out of town were no risk or threat, and they simply wouldn't know what to look for.

Harvey noted the change and shifted gears, "We have a suspicion that the professor somehow manipulated the gaming tables to the Casinos advantage and someone did not want that advantage to go to the other casinos and killed him, Are we anywhere close that possibility?"

Pfeiffer jumped to his feet, the neutral face gone, and his raspy voice in high gear, "You are far off the base, the Professor DID NOT WORK FOR US ALONE, He did the same work for every other casino in town, and His design machines are INDUSTRY standard. In fact every machine in Vegas that is fully automatic comes from his design and comes the manufacturer direct to the casinos, the damn Gaming Board even tells us where to put the machine on the floor, which we may not change without their OK! OK?"

Megan almost sighed in satisfaction, it was nice to get a rise out of this guy, rattle the cage and the beast roars in impotent rage.

Two security guards hearing the raised voice of their boss slipped into the room, they were dressed for the part complete with dark glasses.

"So your machines are no different from the machines at other casinos" this was said in a reconciliatory voice, mollify the guy!

"Absolutely!" the storm had passed; the ship was on even keel now.

Harvey began the next question as though he was considering another possibility. "Or do you think it possible that someone killed him because he was making a lot of money out of the casinos?"

"Lot of money? What are you talking about?" asked Pfeiffer

The answer was crisp "Millions!" Megan could get the attention with that voice of hers.

After a few moments of looking at the two of them, Pfeiffer recovered his poise somewhat "You mean the Don's playing, he was a good player, he was good and had a passion to beat the machines and did that regularly too, but not like the others he played a bit and moved on to other tables and other casinos also all in the same night, there are guys who think playing long at one place gives them better odds but he proved them wrong, anyway you are talking about probably the best brain in the gaming industry, he won so he won, for that nobody's going to go shoot him in his house through the open window".

Harvey and Megan did not have to exchange glances at this remark, they both had registered the 'open window' description from the man, and the quarry was still not in the net. The remark merely registered his knowledge of a fact that they had kept from the media and press, the chief had told the media merely that, the victim had been shot in his study, nothing else.

Harvey tried one more gambit, this one a sly reference to the security guards at their back, "Yeah, he was shot gangland style, and there are no gangs in San Carlos, the professor having this connection in Vegas gave us an idea that may be a gang here had ordered the hit" The implication was obvious your town may have gang members and someone could order a hit!

Pfeiffer hastened to explain, "There are no gangs or the mob in Las Vegas anymore, you are still thinking of the days of Bugsy Siegel, these days it is squeaky clean, the gaming Board has to certify anyone to be employed in a

Casino, any priors and that's it, no entry. You won't find anyone with any connection to a gang. Why a guy has too many parking tickets unpaid and he might kiss his job goodbye."

Megan sensed the door behind them opening and closing, the tough but discrete security had slipped out.

Megan pulled out a small recorder and placed it on the table, "Our next questions are routine, you can answer them or refuse, it is your right to refuse to answer them, please note that at present you are not in custody nor do we have a reason to place you in custody at this time."

Something about an official police caution about self-incrimination gets the goat of most guys. It's like they can't swallow, can't spit.

The first few questions were routine, where were you on Saturday 28th? Here in Vegas at the Casino. Have you ever been to San Carlos? No. What was your relationship with Professor McPherson? He was a patron and a consultant. Did you have cordial relationship with him? Yes. Do you know of any danger that Dr. McPherson faced? No. What is your role in the Casino? I am C.O.O., and Compliance officer, which means I represent the company before the Gaming Board.

Then the fresh unexpected questions, "Is Mr. Bruce Trent in Las Vegas Now?"

"He is in Macau, we are breaking ground on our new casino there" this was said with some relief in his tone.

To the detective duo this was an item to be flagged, 'Glad' the boss is not here? Why?

"Is Mr. Trent the owner of the business?"

"Well, he is a large shareholder"

Megan cutting to the chase, "Who is the largest shareholder?"

Pfeiffer had a sheepish look, obviously he did not know, "We are a Delaware Corporation"

This detail meant nothing to the two of them; it wouldn't have made a difference if he had said 'we are a New Jersey Corporation'. Corporate affairs on the eastern seaboard didn't interest them. East is East and West is West, and never the twain shall meet.

Harvey began to wind up the interview, reciting for the machine the persons present, the time and place, while Megan had fallen silent, she had been racking her brain, things she had read somewhere about the Delaware corporations, suddenly it came to her.

Leaning forward intently she said to Pfeiffer, "We'll never know who the majority shareholder in this company is, will we? Unless someone sues you, for a criminal act!"

Pfeiffer shot up from his seat, "Who's suing us for a criminal act? We operate properly under the laws of Delaware and Nevada and er . . . other states"

"What other states and what business?" Harvey pitched in quickly, giving him no time to formulate an evasive answer. Also at the same time wondering: if they were investigating corporate law violations or a murder.

"We have a fish processing unit in Washington" Pfeiffer seemed low in spirit. He deeply regretted underestimating this cop couple from Redwood City it was in hind sight, a mistake to take them on by himself he should have had a lawyer present from the beginning. He could have taken shelter under the guise that since he was only an employee it would be better that the company's legal counsel be present to answer questions relating to business that he knew nothing about. Come Monday and Bruce would roast him.

Harvey had one last question the one about the money that the Professor had made, "Were you aware if Professor McPherson routinely had winnings of more than ten thousand dollars during his play here?"

This was a hairy question for Pfeiffer, he was aware that Nevada had repealed all laws relating to dealing in cash at the casino, but who knows this could be a federal regulation, particularly the limit, the sum of ten thousand dollars. He hesitated and said firmly "I don't think anyone routinely wins ten thousand at our tables." A safe answer.

They left the place much to the relief of Pfeiffer, who called his boss and related the visit of the cops from Redwood City. Bruce Trent heard his assistant quietly, finally Pfeiffer asked him "You there Boss?"

"Tell them I am held up at Macau for another 10 days, I shall be back in the second week of the month" He abruptly hung up. He had to be careful nowadays, you never know who was listening to your calls, maybe recording it too. He had to wrap up the Game. There were no more plays left for him. He was already the last player left except for his partner.

Chapter 12

THE HEAT IS ON

The cops headed back to the Metropolitan Police Department building, D/C Waller was waiting for them. Harvey led with the briefing, and then converged on the points of interest that had come up during the interview.

He set out in detail Pfeiffer's response and their take on what it might mean.

First was that Pfeiffer feared any connection being made to the work that the professor had done for the Casinos with his murder.

He knew or had guessed that the Professor had made a lot of money, but he seemed unaware of the cash found in the locker.

He had been to the scene of the crime or someone had told him about the shooting through the open window. Otherwise he could not have known of that open window. A fact not made public by the Sheriff's office to anyone.

If he was in fact in the Casino on Saturday the day of the murder then the tapes from the casino would have to be verified for which they would require a warrant and would have to set out probable cause.

He seemed very glad that his boss, Bruce Trent was not there in Las Vegas at the moment answering questions from cops.

He also said that Dr. McPherson did the same kind of work of every other casino in Vega. That his designs are there in practically every gaming machine.

At this Waller laughed and said "Out of Towner's! He considers you out of towers who wouldn't know; Let me tell you that there are thousands of machines in Las Vegas made by dozens of manufacturers. There's no way that all those machines are from one man"

Harvey confessed, "That's our handicap, we know nothing of this industry, can we get to talk to somebody who might give us a primer?"

Waller pointed at her chief of Homicide/Burglary Robert Flake: "there he is the department's resident expert on Gaming Industry and an occasional player".

Harvey and Megan were surprised they had not so far even asked him about gambling and neither had he showed off his expertise.

Waller commanded her deputy "Tell them all about the Board and the approval of the machines and when you finish call me, I will be back to hear more from the only interesting investigation in Las Vegas at the moment."

Captain Flake set about his task of educating them.

"The regulations are enforced by the Gaming Board, the law basically stipulates that a Game, whatever game, Card, Slot, Table Game all should be fair game, A fair game is the one that returns at least 75% of the amount of wagers made on it, I am sure you understand that now. But, Casinos pay out much higher than that, surprised?" he stopped to watch their reaction.

They were truly surprised, until then they had assumed that the Professors value to the Casinos was based on the fact that he had with his expertise saved them money by fixing the machines. This didn't jell with that assumption.

"Yes, they pay more than the minimum to attract players, that is not to say that the casinos are giving away more money, it will appear to a player that he is winning after a few turns at the machine. You see at the slot machine a tourist sits down and starts playing, a few rounds later he hits a win, so continues, if he does not get anything within a few rounds of play he will quit. So the casinos fix it, quite legitimately I might add, to see that there is a pay-out. In Las Vegas the Pay-out percentage would be 90 to 95 percent called return percentage, but if you look at the win% for slot machines of the patrons, it would be 6, 6.5.% at the most. That's the amount that all the patrons win at slot machines. Still the machine is a fair game. That's quite good profit for the Casinos isn't it? The taxable income of Casinos for the whole state would be about 10 billion $! so it does not matter they give away a good chunk to the visitors to have that much left with them."

Having put them wise to the working of casinos and at the same time confusing them as to what the Murder Victim had done for the casinos to have him as a consultant for a good ten years!

And so they asked him "Then what could he have done that benefited the Casinos?"

"Well, that's difficult to even guess, but my bet would be not on the paying percentage but the frequency, pay back to get back! That would be a good strategy for a casino"

"Why is that? Because the winner will take more turns at the same machine?"

"Yes, that the psychology, I think another manipulative tactic would be to fix the jackpots, you see the normal pay out in a slot machine is not much, but the Bonus and Jackpot gives big returns, If the machine were to act, let us say on a signal to give out a Jackpot just as a big group walks in those walk ins are not going to leave!"

But Flake seemed to have doubts about that, "I don't see how they could do it, the Gaming Commission, virtually tears the machine and the controllers apart to find out, the EPROMS, that's the chip comes with designated pay back or known payback percentage, the gaming commission tests those." He shook his head.

Harvey had been mulling over the equation, big money big returns otherwise there would not be such high returns every time, "The Professor would need chips to play just like any other player right? So can we find somehow what stake he would begin with?"

Flake was relieved, this one he could answer, "The casinos have no duty to report any cash transactions large or small to the gaming board, those regulations were repealed some time ago,"

Harvey was surprised, "Why did they repeal the regulations to report large cash transactions?" it seemed most kind of Nevada to facilitate illicit money flow into the gambling industry.

"I don't know, maybe they have different regulations"

Megan asked Flake "WHEN did they repeal those regulations?"

"A couple of years ago, I think, I only remember reading in the papers about it" replied Flake.

Megan was quick to catch on the possibility, "Then they should have records going back earlier to 3 years, this we know has been going on for close to 10 years!"

Flake reached for the phone calling the Gaming Board and connecting with his contact there. After preliminaries he asked do you have records of the previous years when casinos had to report large cash transactions." The answer was apparently positive.

Flake then asked to be put in charge of the section that processed such reports, and was told that the section had been reassigned after the repeal of the requirement.

Flake asked him one more favor, "Just get hold of someone who was there and put me on, they probably would need to have retained the records for some years at least."

After an interminable wait Flake heard someone on the other end explain, Yes the records were preserved and stored, but would need authorization from the Board chief to release the information. Stymied, Flake hung up on her.

Megan combative as ever, urged Flake to report to Waller and seek her assistance. They duly made their way to the chief's cabin and reported. C/D Waller even more assertive than Megan exclaimed, "they want authorization to share information with the County Sheriff's office, ridiculous, here let me call the district attorney, the law is on our side" Waller was confident that she could rely on the District Attorney, a woman of substance, much in her own mould.

Having finished her call, she turned to the expectant detectives and said, "Call the Gaming Board and tell the supervisor in charge of the section, that If the records are not made available to the sheriff's office as of 4.30 this evening the District Attorney is making an application for a warrant to search and seize records that might be necessary in an on-going investigation, a press note will be issued by the Sheriff thereafter"

Harvey was uneasy, it is one thing to try and cut red tape and quite another to go up against the bureaucracy, "Is that necessary?"

Waller was pragmatic enough to have thought through the repercussions, "Actually this is cop's poker, that's why I suggested that a press note is on the way, they won't like the publicity, If they call our bluff there's precious little we can do, in this town the gaming commission and the board are sacrosanct, everyone is scared of them, no member of the senate or the assembly will ever be seen entering a casino for fear they will accused of being cozy with them, Caesar's wife and all that, why even the judge may refuse a warrant and advise us to work in the spirit of cooperation with another arm of government".

Flake picked up the phone and delivered verbatim the threat from his chief to the supervisor. Hanging up he turned to them with a smile on his lips, "The supervisor says Give me a minute!"

The phone rang inside the minute; Flake listened and turned to them, "For what period do you want the records?"

Harvey said, "For five years prior to the repeal of the regulation".

They made their way to a computer and Flake began to download the file that had been sent from the board, having downloaded he couldn't get to open them, Megan stepped up, "Here let me do that" Harvey couldn't resist telling Flake, "Oh! She's good at computers she always playing game on them". Back at Redwood City everyone knew her penchant for playing games at her desk, against every regulation of the department. Fortunately for her the division's computers were isolated from others in the building and the admin guys never set foot in the investigation division.

Megan unable to retort slipped into a seat across the terminal keying furiously she managed to open the files and was staggered to find thousands of records. "Holy smoke, what's this? Does everyone deal only in cash in Vegas?"

Harvey said, "What do you expect, that's about 5 years of records, try and do a search to isolate only the name McPherson".

Even that proved to be formidable, each record a scanned copy of the filing by the casinos for amounts above three thousand dollars each time. It was clear to them that the gaming board had duly received the information as stipulated by the statute. What action the board had taken subsequent to the filing was not clear. File and forget, typical of a bloated bureaucracy.

Flake was disgusted, "If I were a mob guy that's what I would have done, bring in cash, buy chips, pretend to play and then return the chips and ask the casinos would you please remit this to my bank?, that's how I would launder money! Because banks don't have to report remittances but do have to report cash deposits to some federal agency."

Megan interrupted him, "No, No, No, look here at the Transaction reports, this column is for cash inward and this column is for the cash paid out! Even Steven every time, so there goes your laundering theory"

It was Harvey who made the connection, "He pays in the cash, gets the chips and plays, surrenders the exact value back and his winnings he leaves behind for the casino to remit to his bank account, that's what all those remittances we found at the bank!, just think about it, the man made money every time more than his stake and never at a loss! Staggering!"

But what would it prove? It was a sobering thought.

Harvey had to think back as to the other items that he had flagged after his interview with Pfeiffer, "He said they were a Delaware Corporation, Megan here thinks that it is way of hiding the largest shareholder, Is that so?"

"No, Not here the Gaming Commission will require that detail, they may not be in the public domain but definitely will be available with the Commission" and then not wanting to leave anything to chance, "Yes. I suppose so, let me check with Waller, she would know".

"Another thing is the gaming machine can we check with someone in the gaming Board about the machine approval, what did they find or did not find?"

"We can do that right now, they are very open about the testing process, they may not reveal details of proprietary technologies, but the testing is their domain" Flake then led them out.

Soon, Harvey, Megan and Flake found themselves in the large testing lab of the Gaming Board. Attending to them was Peter Grick; Flake introduced the visiting detectives from California and in return introduced Grick as 'Gricktronics of Nevada'. This seemed to please the guy and he put them through the process they followed from the time the machine arrived for testing to its final certification and the specific permit for its location.

The detectives not much interested in the technical angle came to the question that had been on their minds "Could any machine have been programmed to perform as to give undue advantage to the casino?" Grick was puzzled he had spent a good part of the hour explaining that ensuring that the machine were tested for 'Fair' meaning that the return percentage was in the acceptable range. Harvey sensed that the guy was unable to understand what they had come to find, so he began again, "Can an Algorithm, be written in such a fashion that the machine would perform to any one's advantage, not just the casino?"

Grick said, "Of course any one can write an algorithm any ways they want, for one process you can write ten different algorithms!"

"So you are saying that Dr. McPherson could have written an Algorithm to suit the kind of response from the machine and the chip works that way?"

"No they give us the Algorithm themselves it makes life easier for them and us too, If you are looking for game cheats look for simpler devices like the slot machines. That's why all the cheats that were ever caught had something to do with Slot Machines, not Casino Games!"

He stopped however and said "Why do you think we keep so busy, every year we get 50 to 60 new games, I mean New Games, new controls, new controllers, some are old games but are new versions, in each we look for any program or device attached that responds to commands or signals that could affect the outcomes, not once in any have we have found any such thing, any particular manufacturer in mind?"

"Not a manufacturer but gaming mathematicians, Dr. McPherson of California, have you heard of him?"

Grick smiled, he obviously liked the professor, "Yes, quite ingenious his logic programs have been, he could do magic with the numbers, every casino wanted that kind of logic built in, so quite a few casino games bear his imprint, we have tested all of them and they conform to our standards 100%"

Harvey asked him, "Who were the manufacturers using his logic?"

Grick said, "The Manufacturers didn't use his logic, the logic went into the chips, which the manufacturers sourced and used in the games designed by them"

Harvey felt that this was like twenty questions, you had to figure out the correct one to arrive at the truth or no dice, "Who MADE the chips?"

Grick didn't know and said as much, explaining that these were custom chips made in very small batches and major chip makers couldn't do them, so either it had to be made at a lab or someplace like Taiwan, "Look, the numbers are not large, in the state if you have about 5000 casino game stations, a new game would probably be a hundred units, for slot machines of which there may be a hundred, hundred fifty thousand, the new games would be 250 or so, so chips are custom made and are very expensive, that's why the developers are so very nervous when they submit the machines to us, a rejection, they sink!"

Peter Grick sensed that his listeners were a disappointed lot, trying to cheer them up he said, "Come on up here let me show you a chip and game controller from Dr. McPherson, he has a great many fans in the casinos" so saying he led them in to a storage area and pulled out a carton and dug out a chip, a chip on control board like any other in a modern computer. He handed it to Harvey, to who this was no different than any he had ever seen, except that this had an orange color strip across the length and breadth.

Grick continued his commentary, "That orange strip is the signature of the McPherson type of game controller it's a sort of protection against chip malfunction if the circuits heat up for any reason."

"Is that what it does?" Harvey asked, telling himself that it was an irrelevant question; the gaming board would have tested that anyway.

"Yeah, we put it thorough a lot of heat tests, it does protect to some extent, but the chips can't stand heat, they are tropicalized and all that, but leave it in the desert sun for a couple of hours or so and they warp, protection or not"

Harvey held the chip on the palm of his hand it was no bigger than a tablet computer, Megan reached across and took it from him, and said, "The professor was a game math guy and it's all about logic right? What's HE got to do with chips and heat protection?"

The others turned to her in amazement; she might have as well touched off a fire cracker. Harvey's reaction was childish he plucked the chip control board from Megan and waving it asked Grick, "Can we keep this?"

Grick in turn tried to calm the obvious excitement of these detectives, "We would have tested that chip so many ways, I don't think it is functional anymore, there may be many more of those in the casinos still working!"

Harvey said, "But this is my first game chip, I want it" a child not to be denied.

When they returned triumphantly to the Met police office, D/C Donna Waller was flummoxed; she didn't understand their euphoria, "What's with the game control board anyway? It's been tested by the gaming board isn't it?"

"But it doesn't sound right, does it? What's a math prof got to do with Electronic chips and heat protection?" said Flake having caught the fever of excitement from his California counterparts.

Waller didn't know whether that sounded right or not, she couldn't figure out how these detectives from California could stumble upon a chip that seemed to thrill them, "What are you going to do with that chip?"

Harvey assumed an academic air, "We'll test it thoroughly at a lab!"

"But it has been already tested by the gaming board or not?" Waller skeptical.

"Well this chip may not even work; it has been tested so thoroughly that it may not be functional, according to Peter Grick of the board. But we'll be looking at other things"

"What other things?" Waller, looking askance at the three of them, especially at Captain Flake. She meant to convey to Flake that if the Redwood City Sheriff's office solved their homicides this way, it was just fine, but not here in Las Vegas.

Harvey was hesitant to admit complete ignorance, "Actually, I . . . . we don't know, exactly that is, but there are people at the university who should be able to tell us" recalling just in time that this chip may have originated in a Laboratory. Persuading himself that universities do have laboratories that do this sort of work.

Harvey swiftly changed the topic before scorn took firm root in Waller's mind., "We have unfinished business here but nothing we can do independently, the 'person of interest' at the moment is only Bruce Trent and he is away at Macau, in the meantime Captain. Flake can get us the details of the ownership of the Topkapi and also dig up if there is anything to their unrelated business venture, a fish processing unit in Washington."

With any other person, Megan would have struck a pose and said, 'We'll be back', not Waller, who could freeze the blood in your veins.

Flake drove them back to their gratis accommodation, on the way Megan made it clear that she would be willing to head back to Redwood City only in the morning; she wouldn't want to miss her night out in Las Vegas. Harvey concurred wholly and happily. Harvey waited in the lobby for Megan to get ready for the evening. When she appeared Harvey was stunned, she was in a fashionable dress that could only be described as a knock out. Had she packed the dress in anticipation of an evening out with him in Las Vegas? Megan was pleased with his reaction, "Are you ready to escort me, Sir?"

Harvey was glad that he had persuaded Flake to come with them to guide them around the attractions. There's a reason that Doctors are told to have a female nurse present when they examine a female patient. He told her that they had to wait for Flake to come by with his wife. Megan caught the meaning, "You are scared to go with me alone, don't worry women aren't interested in men who they know is interested in another woman". Harvey protested instantly, "That's not true . . . ." What he meant was that he was married and though he WAS interested in Elle, she did not qualify as another woman.

Megan shrewdly exploited the opening that he gave her, "So you are saying that you aren't scared to go out with me and that I am interested in you!"

Harvey was sinking in the quicksand of this woman's logic, fortunately Flake arrived with his wife, and he jumped up to greet them effusively.

Flake proved an able and knowledgeable guide, showing them the sights and the action in the casinos. Harvey remembered Waller telling them that Flake was an occasional player. They were soon caught up in the heady atmosphere of the casinos, everything so designed that visitors forgot everything else except the moment when the dice rolled or the wheel stopped spinning.

Megan a mixture of caution and aggression chose the slot machines, told by Flake that the 5cents slots returns were higher she promptly set about to test the theory, repeatedly feeding the coins and pulling with vigor. When after it had failed to throw up a winner, she muttered rather loudly she was thinking of suing Prof McPherson for intentional deceit. Where is the 95% return percentage on my money she asked Flake plaintively.

Harvey had better luck than his partner, on the American Roulette, a version they called the Action Roulette, he bet big on the 'No Repeat' on 16 rounds at 35-1 odds and it paid off, collecting his winnings, he forgot that this was a stroke of luck, about to chance his arm again Flake held him back and led him away to join the ladies for the dinner.

Harvey sobered up in a hurry and insisted that they have the best food in town, Megan agreed, particularly since Harvey offered to pick up the check. So they ended up at the most expensive place and Megan was content. The Maître appeared and asked if they wanted anything else, Megan said sure, "How can I get on your rating list?" "Rating List to do what?" asked that poor soul.

"To taste the food!"

Chapter 13

BACK TO SCHOOL

The next morning they had to hurry to catch the flight back home, Flake appeared and dropped them at McCarran Airport which was surprisingly close to the hotel, watching the other passengers all bleary eyed, Harvey wondered why they did not stay back for the approaching weekend, maybe there was disapproving spouse back home. Harvey hurried out of his seat and entered the tiny wash room on the plane and splashed cold water on his face hoping his last night excess didn't show on the face. Megan noticed his actions and patted his hands reassuringly telling him no one will know of his debauchery in Las Vegas. But this kind of down sentiment was against her ebullient nature so she assumed the most exaggerated posture and declared, "We'll be back" looking at the ground below of the fast disappearing Las Vegas/Paradise landscape.

Harvey made his way back from San Francisco Airport fearing the disapproving spouse, and Susan did not fail in her role of the tormentor. It is surprising that they pick on the weakest spot without seeming to try thought Harvey as Susan began with, "So you broke the bank in Las Vegas, the family awaits your munificence"

Harvey hurriedly dug into his overnight bag and produced a plastic model of the Bellagio complete with the famed fountain and set it before his son Adam who was having his breakfast cereal. Adam glanced at it disdainfully; Harvey desperately wanted his son to recognize that it was no empty gesture and pointed out to him the impressive features of the Bellagio, "That Lake there, is seven acres across". Adam couldn't have cared less, he walked across the room to the corner and opened the Keyboard of the organ and began to play, and Harvey felt that it was a dirge that people heard when they closed the coffin on the dead.

He himself had resisted the impulse to go down the slippery slope of disdain, initially retaliating with barbs of his own, but virtuously avoided it, telling himself that disdain is like a virus, soon everyone that caught it was . . . . sneering. His diagnosis was proving right the son had the sneer on his face and at the moment he strongly resembled his mother. Harvey mentally ticked off a score card of the progeny 'Like me' and 'Unlike me', he came to the noticeable aspect of his son the profusion of hair, hirsute, the tick went to the distaff side, a 'chromosome contest' he thought wryly and quit the contest even before it had started properly telling himself that Professional Tennis Players did it all the time. Quite like a professional player having received his appearance money, he quit while slightly behind in the game.

Harvey ran upstairs to have a second shower of the morning, and get to work; it was then that he realized that he had left his car in the parking lot of the San Francisco Airport. He and Megan had got on the train at SFO and simply continued, Megan assuming that he had taken the train to the Airport.

Harvey came down and asked if he could get a drop to work, Adam and his mother exchanged a glance and said sure, hop in the back that Adam was going to take the test for the License later in the coming week. Never very argumentative, Harvey sat in the back while his son negotiated the streets carefully, while his mother put out a restraining hand now and then, guiding her son on the onerous duty of getting his father to work without mishap.

Getting off on the opposite side of the county center, he thanked his son for the drop, which was not acknowledged; he trudged the half mile to his office in a better frame of mind.

Arriving he was greeted by the sight of Megan regaling the Division with vignettes from her sojourn in Las Vegas.

They were promptly summoned to the office of Chief Boskey, leaving Las Vegas with a dread of a peer to peer communication between D/C Donna Waller and Chief Boskey of San Mateo Sheriff's Office they were almost sure that last night's conduct of two detective officers had been reported.

The charges against them 'Conduct unbecoming of an officer' a benchmark easily attained by every other officer, compromising an investigation by personal indulgence . . . . ., the professional standards guys would be ready to pound the gavel on those. What is the saying, 'what happens in Vegas, stays in Vegas!' is that going to hold good?

Fearing the worst, they presented themselves. The chief was all smiles, "What have you two done to that lady in Las Vegas? She told me, she never seen two detectives more perceptive than you two!"

Megan was thrilled, "She said that about us? I am not surprised, she's one hell of a boss lady . . . ." then stopped, never compare a female performer with an immediate boss who happens to be a male, Career suicide!

Harvey stepped into the breach, recounting that the visit had yielded a vital clue and they had no idea what that clue would yield except that they had a strong feeling that it meant something big in this whole mystery. Boskey was quite impressed by the determination of the team to get at the working of Dr. McPherson's magic with the casinos.

"The Met police in Vegas helped us a lot, in fact they are working on a few things, we expect to hear from them in a day or too. Something is not right about the Casino Topkapi, but can't say what! The chief of operations there is a strange character, one moment he is all calm and the next he gets rattled. The ownership of the casino is what the Met police are going to find, that should give us some clue. We can be certain that McPherson manipulated the Casino machines somehow, just to what extent and if there are others are involved is hard to say. Pfeiffer definitely has some information on the shooting here, he mentioned the open window and that was a giveaway, which he can deny at a later date as just a figure of speech."

Harvey the told the chief the next steps they planned to take "Right now our biggest task is to find what that chip does, especially the heat protection strip".

Boskey himself had something to report that he had ordered surveillance of the McPherson residence and that 'Joey&Joey' had a tough time as that neighborhood had no traffic and virtually no cars parked at the kerb and that the team was forced to do a drive-by surveillance that did not yield anything of value. Except that a van bearing the insignia of a local satellite company had arrived and dismantled a small dish and drove away.

The team, Devlin with prior exposure to the subject, with Taggart adding the gravitas, that had forayed into the University had fared no better, Dr. Murphy had proven impervious to the presence of a senior in the team, and it had all been barbs and taunts. Taggart began his briefing with the pithy observation that the subject was "Loony" he might as well have said that the subject was an 'Asshole'. The emphasis was clear, as if confirm his strong view in the matter he looked to chief Boskey, the chief nodded diplomatically, he having come up the ranks with the firm view that it is generally that assholes are nabbed and not loony subjects. Squeamish PR machinery had decreed that the subjects be referred to as subjects and not as "Loony' or 'Asshole' etc. The exact directives would be found in the manual specially prepared for serving officers to reform those who had inculcated this attitude; this was presumed to be any one over the age of 25.

According to Taggart, Dr. Murphy was erratic and appeared confused at times but for the greater part was lucid and articulate. He did not answer questions regarding his location at the approximate time of the murder. Devlin had recorded the exact response 'I might have been in the loo the whole time doing the damn crossword'.

Was Dr. Murphy aware of the work of Dr. McPherson for the Casinos?"

"Oh!, Yes, quite naturally he has told me all the things that go on in Las Vegas, I tell you, some people go to work to earn money, other go to Las Vegas, You are the detectives, tell me, why would he go to Vegas and not go to work?, my advice is look for the obvious, did he need the money? I will answer that for you NO!"

Dr. Murphy then launched into a monologue on gambling, it was as if the cops weren't even there, "Gambling is not a vice, it's not a habit, it's a disease that disrupts the neurons in the brain, it feeds voraciously on the dream of the losers, it upsets the calculus of life, no more boring infinitesimal accretions, you win and bang life is different! Lose and you are regarded as problem gambler but the truth is that he is but a chronic patient, the only cure is a solution to the losing streak, win and win surely, Dennis did it, but his solution he took to his grave, why he refused to share I will never understand"

Then in an dramatic shift of mood Dr. Murphy said "He didn't tell me anything, I begged him to write it down and publish one book on the subject, I told him even that if his method became universal, there are or there would be others, to overcome it, but he refused, by his silence he brought about his own death, the ultimate writer's cramp".

Taggart & Devlin, thoroughly confused by the mad professor had made their way out of the department.

The team debated what to do about the seemingly unstable professor, Boskey then directed that Taggart and Devlin would tail him for a couple of days. A routine that did not hold much hope of turning anything worthwhile in the probe, but Devlin was pleased that he could spend the next two days at least in the university campus a veritable picnic!

Harvcy and Megan then hurried to get to the Coroner's office for the inquest. A small gathering in the coroner's court awaited them, They knew it was a formality, the Medical examiner, in this case, the Crime Lab had already certified the cause of death as a gun shoot wound to the head. The Coroner pronounced that details and added it was classified as a Homicide by unknown person/persons.

Outside Harvey met with Elle and Miriam, there were a few things that Harvey wanted to ask her and it felt awkward to do that in front of Elle. Overcoming his hesitation he asked her anyway, "In your interview you said that ever since the money came in from Las Vegas your fears had increased, what money was that?"

Miriam didn't have to recollect what she had said at the interview, she had a bad feeling about the money ever since Dennis had told her about it, "I don't know how much money, but Dennis said it was a lot!, he said they sent him the money to play freely with it in the casino, I asked him why would they give him the money to play?, he said something about a track record and that it wasn't going to fool anybody, but he wouldn't tell me anything more"

Elle who had followed the conversation nodded slightly at Harvey signaling that Miriam wouldn't have known any more than that.

"Dennis wasn't afraid, but he became withdrawn and stopped going to Vegas, saying that he was no longer doing any consulting"

And then the unexpected, "Do you know anything about a couple of file cabinets that were in the basement?"

Harvey distinctly remembered that there were no file cabinets in the basements. "What file cabinets?"

Miriam told him that the last time she was home in the summer there had been two file cabinets in the basement, which had always been there since long. She said that she had checked with Tilden from the Crime Lab who said that they had not removed any cabinets from the house and had faxed her the entire list of the items removed from the house. No cabinets.

Harvey asked her "Did you know what was in them?"

"one had files something to do with Dennis' work for the casinos and the other had some odds and ends with electronics, Dennis always kept them locked" Miriam wasn't very sure of it.

Harvey turned around to find Megan at his side with a smug look on her face; it was a look that he knew too well. "What?"

Megan of the smug mug, "You'll know about those File cabinets in say about an hour at the most"

Harvey had obviously missed an investigating trick, "How?"

"I called the District Attorney's office" smug satisfaction very pronounced.

"Why would the District Attorney's office know where a couple of File Cabinets are?"

"Because the DA's office has been working overtime in cracking down on illegal movers all over California, they have even arrested a bunch of them so that all moving companies are very cooperative with the DA's office, one call from the office and they move, that's a pun by the way, you know moving companies moving?"

Confidence breeds confidence, Harvey turned to Miriam and told her grandly "You will know about your missing File Cabinets in an hour"

Miriam was duly impressed by the efficiency of the cops and hoped that they would be as successful in tracking her husband's killer. She invited them to the wake for her husband the next day.

"An Irish wake?" asked Megan, a California child who hadn't been to a funeral in her life. Everyone in her family was long lived her great grandmother was approaching the century mark and drove her motorized wheelchair dangerously around the malls.

"No" Miriam told Megan, "A Scottish wake, I suppose it's the same thing, we have short memorial service, then the funeral and lunch is at the parish hall in the church"

Harvey and Megan then headed straight to the university their first point of contact would be the voluble Patrick Diggs. Megan was in a chatty mood asking Harvey, "Fancy that! A Scottish wake and funeral, do you think they will have bagpipers playing?"

Harvey was horrified, "I hope not!" he had heard bags being played and had no wish to repeat the experience. He remembered it from Arlington national cemetery; all those gravestones had not depressed him as much as the bags they played, the bagpipes were a perfect lament for the dearly departed.

Megan was not done, "You know what they say, after attending a funeral, couples invariably make passionate love! I have read about it"

Harvey pleaded with her, "Will you please stop this chatter of useless tidbits! Who wrote that bit of garbage? He follow couples home from a funeral and peep?"

"Jeez, he wouldn't have to peep, it's common knowledge, some candid confessions, one person tells another, and another, it's like the six degrees of separation between every person on this planet, same thing with information, I told you now, you tell another and soon everyone knows, it becomes common knowledge. Peeping! Jeez that's just like all the guys driven by salacious thoughts"

Not driven by salacious thoughts but definitely driven to distraction he decided to stop his partner from continuing, "So what you planning for tomorrow, bringing your husband to the funeral and . . ." he didn't finish Megan had delivered a swift punch which left his arm numb.

They were not making much progress on the road to the university, traffic was crawling and at every intersection on El Camino they were at a complete stop, soon they saw the cause of the hold up a big Beer truck had somehow jack-knifed across the road, Megan noticed the green colored sides of the truck showing Carlsberg beer cans, "I like Carlsberg Beer"

Harvey had to challenge that, "What's wrong with Bud?" loyal to the American brand.

Megan had to stick to her choice, "Bud is a Vegan Beer, besides they once sued Denzel Washington and he did not win an Oscar!"

Harvey was amazed at this woman's fund of trivia, "Why did they sue Denzel Washington? He refuses to drink it? Or what they sue him so that he doesn't win an Oscar?" "Megan did not know, "I don't actually know if they sued, but he did not win an Oscar" apparently trivia does not go into the details.

Harvey dug into his own memory "Yes, he did, Denzel Washington has won an Oscar everybody knows that".

A peremptory challenge from Megan, "When?"

Harvey had to shake his head; his trivia too apparently did not deal with details.

Eventually they arrived at the university and Harvey with his knowledge of the location of the building parked closer to it and they entered the department and Patrick Diggs greeted Harvey cordially. Harvey prepared himself for the verbal onslaught he knew was coming.

Megan, he knew, would develop a natural affinity for this gabby Assistant Professor.

Patrick did not fail his expectation, "So what are you looking at now, no more paradoxes? I actually looked up paradox after you left it's amazing how many have developed over the years, it's mostly imprecisely stated propositions, causes one to look like a mug trying to answer them. In very large numbers they are very complicated. Way beyond me to explain them. So what can I help you with now?"

Harvey wordlessly produced the game chip from Vegas and placed it on the table in front of the junior don. "Is that a game controller from a gaming machine, it's the first time that I have seen one" said Patrick.

Harvey's turn to be surprised, "I thought you told me that you had been to Las Vegas to test the machines?"

"Ah, I tested the logic, which means I write up a program to perform the same functions as the professor's logic framework, and test for residuals and loops, you know circular functions and things like that, I did not work with chips or controllers"

Megan asked him, "So you can't tell us what this thing does?"

Patrick rubbed his chin "It controls the game, assuming that it is from a gaming machine, do you know which game this is from, maybe then I can hazard a guess as to the functions, not precisely but generally"

Harvey and Megan did not know which gaming machine this chip had come from. It had not occurred to them to ask the Gaming Board guy. So they asked him what the big difference between one chip and another is.

Patrick was more clear now, "Look there are officially about 750 different gaming machines approved by the gaming commission, so there you have 750 different type of chips all of them controllers and some have some accounting functions too, so if you tell me this is from an American Roulette machine then I can tell you what features or functions that it is supposed to carry out, why did this particular chip interest you?"

Megan reached across and pointed to the bright orange strip running across the length and breadth of the chip, "That's why!"

Patrick picked up the chip and peered closely at it, "How is this linked to Dr. McPherson?"

"All the chips that had this orange thing are supposed to be particular to the games logic by Dr. McPherson. It is supposed to act as some sort of heat shield or prevent game malfunction due to heat"

Patrick made up his mind, "Let's ask the electronics guy!" saying that he rose and gestured to them to follow him. He strode out of the building and Megan quite easily kept pace, Harvey found the pace a bit challenging. Fortunately the Information systems lab was only a short distance and they entered and waited in the foyer while Patrick went in search of a faculty he knew.

They were eventually asked to enter a lab and the young man who they met was introduced as Dr. Trapps a bit young to be a full professor at the university. Dr. Trapps was more reserved than Patrick and examined the Chip for several minutes and then took a peek at it under a microscope.

The detectives decided to let Patrick handle the question, Patrick asked "What's that?" that's a question they could have managed themselves.

Dr. Trapps said "It is a polymer coat printed on the Board, it is not a conductor see it is covering some of the printed circuit on the Board. But it is printed in some sort of pattern, it would be interesting to see the observe side. Can I cut this up?"

"Sure" Harvey said "That piece is probably not functional anyway"

Dr. Trapps asked Harvey, "Why is it not functional?"

Harvey gave him a brief on the origin of the Chip & Board and how it had been subject to tests by the Gaming Commission and the labs that approve the machines and likely rendered it useless.

Dr. Trapps was doubtful, "Tests don't destroy a functional chip and control board, and these are tough babies, only physical damages render them dysfunctional, so let's do some stealth work on this" He then realized that the stealth bit meant nothing to the detectives or even for the Stats guy and told them, "What I meant is we do stealth dicing, cut out a wafer thin layer of the board and take out a piece of the polymer strip"

They were led deeper into the lab and Dr. Trapps fixed the control board on to a frame and slid it into a chamber of a large machine, explaining to them, "The laser works in the chamber but you can see the process on this screen here, but please wear your protective glasses at all times" So saying he switched on the machine and the screen came alive to show a thin beam of light focus on the edge of the polymer strip, a minute and it was done, a thin layer of the material separated from the board. Dr. Trapps brought out the Board and the separated strip of material and then examined it under a large microscope.

He turned to them, "Just as I thought, there is pattern printed on the underside of the strip, a coil like design that runs in a series along the whole length of the strip, to what purpose I cannot say, since this is obviously a non-conducting material"

Megan remembered reading something about polymers, "Don't polymers have some electrical applications?"

"Lots of them" said Dr. Trapps "there are everyday applications of polymers in electrical devices, in capacitors, as insulators, quite a lot actually, in the last 50 years or so, it's a young science and newer applications are being discovered everyday"

Megan was skeptical, "So that's it? It is a decorative piece, a colorful signature of Dr. McPherson?"

Dr. Trapps was thoughtful, "No, I wouldn't say that, you see you can change a polymer by doping it, you can quite dramatically alter its characteristics, and polymers are very versatile materials, it can be changed from crystalline to amorphous and vice versa, but let's see this more closely" and he then placed it yet another machine explaining this was a transmission electron microscope.

He brought it upon a large screen and looked at it for some time then he turned to them and pointed at the image and said, "See those things, those tiny structures are Nano tubes, most probably Carbon Nano tubes, What I can tell you now is that the Polymer like substance is not doped but the Nano tubes are embedded in it, and most likely it is the Nano Tubes that are doped, think of the Nano tubes as sausage skin and you stuff some material into them, in reality they are actually grown in high temperatures and since it is found in a circuit I can only guess that the doping is to change its conductivity."

Megan too curious now to contain herself asked the young professor, "It is on a board and that board will have a constant electric flow and that would alter its conductivity, right?"

Dr. Trapps agreed, "Yes it is on a circuit board and electricity flowing through any circuit will have an electromagnetic field around it. But once the material is exposed to that electromagnetic field it would reach a steady state and change only if something dramatic happens such as application of heat, a strong inductive current, a large magnetic field anything that will cause it to behave differently, change its characteristics and in turn it will cause the circuit board itself to alter in its functions. I think it could be a strong magnetic field applied for duration and once that is switched off the material will return to its steady state"

Dr. Trapps had come to a decision and told them, "I think we will have to use OOMMF to get at that possibility"

Megan heard that as 'Oomph', "You mean Oomph as in Starlets?" wonder in her voice.

For the first time since they arrived Dr. Trapps broke his reserve and smiled broadly, "No, not Oomph as in starlets, But OOMMF program to do magnetic modeling" and then he spelt the acronym for them Object. Oriented. Micro. Magnetic Framework. "Software of a different kind!" he added mischievously.

Harvey heaved a sigh of relief he had visions of cleavage baring starlets teaching him about carbon Nano tubes, still he had to concede it would be a terrific temptation for a student to learn about Nano Tubes, magnetic or not.

Grinning Megan invited them, "Let's get this Oomph, who's got Oomph around here?"

Dr. Trapps, now entirely under the spell of this police woman, offered to find someone in the lab who could guide them and left.

While they waited, Patrick said that he was surprised that Dr. Trapps was being so cooperative with police investigation. It was well known around the campus that he detested cops, stemming from an incident when a couple of cops had stopped him riding his bike for some traffic violation, incensed that his personal decision to avoid the use of a car wasn't being appreciated, he then and there launched into a lecture on using renewable energy and told them that a mere 5 million roof top solar for homes and a half million roof top for big buildings would mean there would be no need to build new power plants burning up imported oil or coal in California, the cops had scooted fearful of this modern day sun god worshipper, a few students were witness to the incident and soon it became campus legend.

Dr. Trapps returned having successfully enlisted someone in the Information Systems Center, "We'll send the material to NIST that is National Institute of Standards & Technology, who can identify the doped material, and they have a database of materials used in labs around the world"

They left the place but not before Megan had effusively thanked the young professor Dr. Trapps who couldn't have been happier if they had nominated him for a Nobel Prize.

On the walk back with Patrick Diggs to his department, Megan got a call on her cell phone, the DA's office had come through on the missing File Cabinets, the moving company had reportedly delivered them to the University at Dr. McPherson's office.

They hurried to the office of Dr. McPherson to find this secretary of many years tidying up the office for a new occupant. She readily recalled that the File Cabinets had been delivered some weeks ago and that there had been a flap about it from security, Dr. McPherson himself had to come down to certify that it was his personal research material and that it contained no hazardous substance.

The file cabinets were like any other, the secretary opened one with a key, it contained bunches of old papers, bundles that had obviously aged discolored and curling at the edges. Megan flipped through one bunch and asked what language is this, is this olde' world' English?

Harvey peered over her shoulder, "That's Slovene!" he said firmly, happy in his knowledge. Megan ever alert to leg being pulled turned on him, "You are kidding!", "Nope!" Harvey secure now that he had outflanked his partner. "So, what's it about?" Harvey studied the text and pronounced "It's about polymers" and pointed to the text that said 'polimer' Patrick joined in the discovery process, "Yep! Definitely Slovene and it's also about Magnets!" and helpfully pointed to the text that said 'Magnetic'. Megan had to agree there indeed were the words polimer and magnetic in that text. The very things they had heard in the Information Systems Lab in the past hour.

"So, tell me genius, how did you know that it is Slovene, you studying European languages on the sly?" Megan might as well have warned him "FESS UP!" Harvey admitted that Miriam had told him that the Professor had been to Slovenia and that it was only now that he was connecting the dots.

The second File Cabinet was a mess of small electronic parts; it was as if a child had dismantled an electronic device. Harvey picked up a small glass tube, "What's this? He asked Patrick.

"I guess that it is a vacuum tube, a miniature one, like those things you had in the radios, only much smaller" he was puzzled "Nobody has any use for these anymore, it is all semi-conductors now"

Megan shifted attention to the lower drawers and found a variety of lighters, there were very many of them. "Did the Professor smoke?" she asked them, Harvey did not know, Patrick said, "No, not here in the University, but he enjoyed lighting up his cigars on the Casino floor, in Las Vegas you can pretty much light up anywhere except a few no go areas, but I did not know that he collected Cigarette lighters a strange hobby for the twenty first century"

Patrick then offered to remove the papers in the file cabinet to the Digital language lab and have it transliterated and when ready they could show it to Dr. Trapps, who would interpret the text for them.

Harvey and Megan made their way back to the car, Megan sighing in satisfaction, "Pretty good day at school!" feeling scholarly.

Chapter 14

THE CERTAINTIES:
DEATH AND TAXES

The next morning Harvey was early at his station, it had been four days and his murder book had nothing in it, it was de ri.gueur for a detective to maintain an hour by hour record of the progress of an investigation if not a minute by minute one. He had a lot of catching up to do. He created four pages for the four days and divided each into hourly intervals starting at 6 o'clock in the morning and ending at midnight, detectives do need to sleep. He began to fill in the activities and findings at each hour going back and forth as he recollected the events and had a fairly easy time. The materials taken from the house of the victim he didn't list, the details could come from the crime lab manifest.

The turn of the investigation after the discovery of the cash hoard in the bank and the CPA accounts he recorded. It established the very real possibility of the professor's penchant for gambling as a motive for murder. The misgivings as to the role of Pfeiffer of

Topkapi casino and the need to follow up and the involvement of the Las Vegas Metropolitan police in the investigation was also mentioned. The last entry would enable them to get search warrants easily now that there is a probable cause in the murder book.

The findings so far as to the possible use of contraband device to cheat casinos and the pending conclusions of the analysis he mentioned but indicated that it did not appear germane to the murder itself. Whatever the professor had done it was clear that he had made illegal gains but paid taxes on it and so did not warrant transferring the case to federal jurisdiction. That decision would have to be made in Las Vegas jurisdiction where the crime had taken place but who would they indict as accused, the main actor was dead!

As he finished up and printed out the murder book, Megan arrived, dressed to kill in all black, seeing her Harvey realized that they were due at the McPhersons for the wake and funeral. Luck was on his side he had worn a regular but black suit. He would not be out of place there.

They then began their regular brief to the Lieutenant Boskey, who listened without interrupting and had a small word of praise for their initiative and insight, the thing left unsaid was the complete absence of a suspect. In the excitement of following up promising leads they had yet to focus on identifying any suspect. There was no one on the radar.

Taggart and Devlin arrived after a night long vigil outside the home of Dr. Murphy, the report was short and baffling, the 'Looney' had entered his home where he lived alone and after sometime turned out all the lights in the house and it remained that way through the night. They had asked a patrol team to keep an eye and would resume the surveillance later.

Harvey and Megan left the building and in the parking lot met Megan's husband waiting for them, Harvey went "Oh! Yeah!" in mock recall of Megan's take on funerals and love, Megan shot him a stern look Harvey pretended to be mortified, soon Megan began giggling. Jacob didn't get the joke between his wife and her partner but was happy for them to be sharing a good bond in such a stressful job.

They arrived at the house of McPherson's to find a large crowd spilling on to the street. They made their way into the house to meet with the widow and son. The gathering was not somber as Harvey had feared but quite social and he heard some people recount some anecdotes of the dead professor. The time came to leave for the church, the detectives learnt that McPherson was a lapsed Catholic in that he wasn't regular in church but he was an active supporter of several church initiatives and well regarded in the community.

They arrived at the beautiful church that had a modern design rather than the regular steeple dominated theme. Harvey spent his time during the service admiring the stained glass windows they too were very different than any that he had seen. The stained glass windows were all high up on the wall and he had to tilt his head to look up to them, the Reverend now then asked them to bow their heads and Megan had to stomp on his feet to get his attention.

Harvey had not been paying much attention to what was being said, until he heard a clear and ringing voice of the speaker who seemed to be in the grip of a powerful emotion, rather than just praise Dr. McPherson the speaker listed the projects that he had been involved in, the humanitarian efforts led by him seemed to span the world, reaching out the hungry and the needy, the sick and the disaster struck people. It left no doubt in any one's mind that the late Professor was a benefactor to countless people.

They left in a convoy of cars to the cemetery and Harvey and Megan agreed that it was best that the man was being laid to rest with his secrets intact and it was not tainted by the knowledge that he may have acted criminally for years. The relief they felt was at odds with the contempt they generally felt toward the criminal.

They returned to the parish hall for lunch and all the guests seemed to take part in serving and managing one another. This was no formal lunch but a family gathering. Harvey did not want to actively seek out Elle but kept his eyes on her movement among the guests and when she spotted him she came to him without the show of formality. Harvey introduced her to Megan and her husband Jacob after a moment Elle held his hand and excusing herself led him to a corner. "Thank you for not telling Miriam about what you have found, I wanted him to have the dignity and love of his family, it would have shattered her to learn anything else"

Elle did not press him of the details of his visit to Las Vegas and Harvey was glad that he did not have to tell her any more of the distressing details. Eventually the family would learn of the truth and accept it. At the moment all that mattered was that a good man, essentially a good man, may have gone to his final resting place loved and cherished as he had undoubtedly been loved and cherished through his life. It mattered little that he had succumbed to an irrepressible need to gamble and win, win at all costs and it may have cost him his life.

They returned to the county center and in the parking lot, Megan said that she would make a quick run home to change to work clothes and get back. Harvey rolled his eyes suggestively and quickly leapt out of the way of the arm that was swinging his way, continuing the momentum he ran into the building leaving Megan to do some explaining to her husband.

On the floor of the department he met a distinctly morose looking team of Taggart and Devlin. They had some bad news. Dr. Murphy was not home and at present not traceable. They had resumed the stake out in the morning relieving the patrol team and after a time, Devlin had curiously rounded the house and found no movement inside the house, stepping up to the front door he rang the doorbell, no one answered. He quickly ran back to Taggart in the car and told him, they rang the home phone of Dr. Murphy again no answer, they called the University and got the news that the Professor had left early the previous day and had not been seen. He had missed a faculty meeting of late, but that had not been considered unusual.

Harvey led them into Lieutenant Boskey's cabin, they debated whether they should issue an APB, but an All-points Bulletin was a sure way of announcing it to the media. Too many people were involved in covering the exits at Airports, Trains to maintain any sort of secrecy. In the end Boskey made the decision to issue the APB, If Dr. Murphy was on a private visit anywhere he would turn up and the department could issue an apology for a hasty notice. But if he did not turn up and he was really on the lam then they had a problem on their hand.

Megan bustled into the cabin; clearly she had heard the APB on the radio. They had the very difficult task of waiting. Harvey decided to call Tilden at the Crime Lab to see if they had turned up anything in all the stuff they had removed from the house of the victim. Tilden was not abreast of the investigation, but the money and the details of the victim's financials that had been analyzed were with him and he had some clue as to the issues involved. Harvey briefed him on the progress of the case particularly the possibility that the Dr. McPherson may have found a way to cheat the Casinos of a large sum of money. Tilden listened with increasing fascination particularly the detail that the university guys are looking to the possibility that the Game Chip and Board had somehow had been manipulated. Harvey then said that he was amazed that no one had known the professor to be an inveterate gambler, a gambling addict, a man who had made millions out of the casinos at Las Vegas, plus he had a stash of a cool ten million in his bank locker, as a man who smoked cigars and collected lighters and not one had a clue to these things for over a decade!

At the remark that the Professor collected Lighters, Tilden became excited, "Listen, that's your clue, he might have built a way to circumvent the game machines operations, but he had to have something to switch on the alternative run of play, a device in hand that would escape attention, what better than a lighter. He must have been using the lighter modified to activate his program, where are the lighters now?"

Harvey told him that they were in the office of the professor at the university and he would get the things to Tilden shortly. Megan was adamant that she would not approach Judge Brewster again for a warrant to remove the personal effects of the professor from his university office; her last experience had not been good. She remembered that the judge was a Stanford alumnus and would likely refuse to sign the warrant, cops violating the privilege of the university! She suggested that Harvey should call Miriam and ask her to call the University office to permit the removal of the personal effects of her husband it would work like a charm.

Harvey called and Miriam was wonderfully cooperative, he skillfully avoided lying to her and merely said that having traced the File Cabinets he wanted to move them to the county's custody. Taggart and Devlin went out to execute the transfer.

An hour later the call came regarding the first information on Dr. Murphy, he had as of yesterday morning arrived at San Carlos Airport, filed a flight plan for McPherson owned Gulfstream 540, for which he had flying privileges, naming himself as Pilot and the necessary permission to land at Henderson Executive Airport at Las Vegas. He had then departed San Carlos at 12.00 hrs. Headed to Las Vegas and Henderson Executive Airport Control Tower reported that the plane had landed without incident and was still parked there.

Harvey then called Captain Flake at Las Vegas and recounted the trace placed on Dr. Murphy and the information that he had indeed landed at Las Vegas, though at the much smaller Henderson Executive Airport. Flake also had information to give Harvey, "We have someone missing here too, Pfeiffer is missing since yesterday morning, the staff at the casino says they have no idea as to his whereabouts but with the threat of prosecution for obstruction we have now obtained a possible location, a house that he occasionally uses. But meanwhile your investigation has had vast unexpected consequences here, you better get here pronto, the brass here is on tenterhooks"

Boskey, told that his team's investigation had touched off a furor in Las Vegas was unwilling to accept any unjustified imputation of wrong doing and decided to call Donna Waller at Las Vegas Metropolitan Police. Boskey merely asked her if Harvey and Megan during their investigation had created a situation for the Met police, Waller was quick to understand his anxiety and assured him that it was not the case at all, merely that the course of the probe had led to unexpected consequences for all the Casinos. It was a Federal Tax matter unconnected to the murder of Dr. McPherson. She added that up until this time only the Met police were aware that the murder probe had indirectly resulted in the Tax matter coming up with the IRS. No one else in the Government was made known of this fact. They had decided to keep it under wraps but it would help matters if the missing professor from the University and the Casino manager Pfeiffer were both traced and some resolution obtained in the case.

Having decided to leave for Las Vegas right away, Harvey and Megan picked small overnight bags from the lockers in the basement and headed to San Francisco airport. On the way the two puzzled over what could have led their probe into the murder to result in an IRS action against all the casinos. They had not discussed the tax matter or anything related to tax with anyone except Flake and that was limited to the murder victim's records' which were 3 years old!

They landed as dusk was falling in that desert city as they emerged from outside the terminal they were pleasantly surprised to find Capt. Flake waiting for them; it was not until they were in the car heading to the Met police office that Flake spoke of the latest development. Pfeiffer had been found dead, shot in the head. It was at the address provided by someone from the staff who was aware of the secret hideout of his boss. The Coroner had said that the victim had been dead at least 24 hours. That would be sometime after 1.00 p.m. yesterday, a time that could possibly put Dr. Murphy at the scene going by the time of his arrival in Las Vegas. A person of interest in the murder of Dr. McPherson was now a possible suspect in the murder of Pfeiffer.

At the Metropolitan Police office they were informed that a two man detective team had been put on the Pfeiffer murder by Capt. Flake, the detectives had been taken into confidence on the possible link to the murder in San Mateo County California.

A meeting was already on in the office of D/C Waller several others present there seemed to be the 'Brass' as Flake had called them. The arrival of the detectives from California stopped their discussion they moved to a briefing room to accommodate everyone.

Invited to go first, Harvey felt at a disadvantage they knew something that he did not know and to explain the progress of a case in his jurisdiction that seemed to have no connection to whatever had transpired here at Las Vegas was a bit much. Gathering confidence that they had not in any way committed a blunder, he set out the findings in California: The help of the University in studying the Gaming Chip and Control Board, the analysis that pointed to a possible way to manipulate the Gaming Machine. "It's not clear at the moment what purpose is served by the polymer strip that seems so harmless. A National Agency is examining the materials used we should have an answer soon. But it is clear from the records that the murder victim in California has scored a big amount from casinos in Vegas that too, over ten years and has gotten away clean. He paid his taxes too."

He waited expectantly for questions but the Met police had none, so he assumed that they were satisfied that he and the team had worked in the right direction.

Waller told him and the others in the room, "The homicide in California is somehow connected to the casinos here, the problem for us is that it seems to involve a substantial number of casinos, the likelihood of which is hard to believe, and perhaps they were all victims of fraud played by the murder victim. Detective Harvey here had told me that he had strong suspicion of the role played by Topkapi Casino, the interview with Pfeiffer threw up a number of questions. A strong indication was the knowledge of Pfeiffer of the fact that the Victim was shot through an open window a piece of information that the San Mateo Sheriff's office had withheld from the public. I had Captain Flake here pursue the investigation here, one the ownership of the casino, the other to put pressure on Pfeiffer by letting him know that we were nosing around. Sure enough Pfeiffer went missing as of yesterday. The records with the Gaming Commission showed that Bruce Trent to be the majority shareholder both of the casino and the holding company. Trying to get to the bottom of that has landed us in this situation"

Harvey and Megan were no wiser after this brief than earlier. Waller gestured with her hand telling them that the details were coming.

Captain Flake stepped forward and began his narration of the events, "Since the Detectives expressed doubts about the affairs of Topkapi, We decided to direct our probe in that direction, first we got the records of the gaming commission relating to the Ownership, there had been no change recorded in the ten years since the license was granted. The public filings of the holding company for the last couple of years also did not give us anything. It is at that point that we turned to FinCEN."

At this point Captain Flake had to do some explaining to the two detectives. The repeal of the provisions in Nevada with regard to reporting of cash transactions of a certain value had been done as that requirement was covered by the Bank Secrecy Act which meant that Casinos had to file the Cash Transactions Report to the 'Financial Crimes Enforcement Network' FinCEN for short.

They did help the Metropolitan Police to confirm that they had tracked a transaction of a Foreign Bank to which the shares of the Topkapi's Holding Company had been shown as pledged. FinCEN had been tracking that issue to unearth the people behind the funds suspecting them of money laundering. They had found that using that security the bank had advanced loans and in satisfaction of the transaction had assigned the shares to another company which was now the beneficial owner of the Casino, a Fact that had not been disclosed to the Gaming Commission in Nevada. After getting this information the Met Police could inform the Gaming Commission and initiate action against Topkapi for violation of Nevada gaming Laws.

It was the next request to FinCEN that triggered the tsunami that was sweeping towards Nevada—the land locked desert state was going to drown in Tax demands!

Captain Flake continued in a tone suggesting 'you won't believe this!' "We asked FinCEN for details of Cash

Transaction Reports for McPherson over the last three years, we got that and no surprises the patterns was the same as with the filing for earlier years with the Gaming Board. The FinCEN guy said he was surprised that this McPherson guy had played so many years yet had not lost any money, the money he paid in and the money paid out was equal!, I told him that was not correct, the guy had made money and paid taxes on it too, the casinos had without fail deducted the withholding taxes. The matter should have ended there but some smart guy ran the CTR of all casinos through their powerful computers and sent in the details to The Internal Revenue Service! It's the IRS which has come up with demand for taxes which by some estimates is in millions! I can't understand why FinCEN which tracks money laundering sent this to IRS for Taxes" with IRS".

Megan was angry and wanted to know, "The Patriot Act is against terrorism isn't it? Now the government is using Patriot Act to go after tax dodgers?"

The 'Top Brass' was amused and indulgent towards this forthright and intelligent cop, "No, Patriot Act merely improved the way information is shared between government agencies and so this bit of information went out to the IRS, nothing sinister about it, By the way, do you know what the full title of Patriot Act is?"

Nobody in that room had an answer, so he informed them, "It's UNITING AND STRENGTHENING AMERICA BY PROVINDING APPROPRIATE TOOLS TO RESTRICT INTERCEPT AND OBSTRUCT TERRORISM ACT—acronym USA PATRIOT ACT."

"Awesome" said Megan impressed "Do we know the name of the worthy who proposed this in the house or senate?"

The 'Top Brass' had a word of appreciation for Megan, "You know, what you said about Tax Dodgers is absolutely right, FinCEN may have sent it as routine Money Laundering info, but for the IRS to use it for any other purpose may be prohibited, the IRS may be the Outlaw in this case, how about that? I'll definitely bring this to the notice of the Gaming Commission; we have to protect our local industry!"

D/C Waller had a word of caution to them all, "Right now nobody knows that it was our enquiry that touched off the IRS investigation into Withholding Taxes by the casinos, let's keep it that way."

The "Top brass' had some words of comfort to the detectives, "The information that I have is that at present the Casino companies are hanging tough, the IRS had sent in requests for information on the number of visitors, the reported Gross Revenue of the companies, steps taken by them to comply with money laundering provisions such as record keeping on repeat visitors who have been included in the Cash Transaction Reports, the casinos are arguing that all these are regularly filed with Gaming Board and they had no requirement of reporting repeat visitors and have no system in place to aggregate winnings of such visitors. In the meanwhile continue with the good work you are on the right track"

The visiting detectives went back with Captain Flakes to his office, the detectives on the Pfeiffer team called in a report to say that they had established that Pfeiffer left the Casino last morning by foot and was seen walking towards the Bonneville Transit Centre so he might have taken the Henderson & Downtown Express to reach a stop down south east and walked to his house. His car is missing from the house. The detectives had also been to the Henderson Executive Airport and no one there remembers when and how Dr. Murphy left the Airport. They were still working on the possibility that Pfeiffer met Dr. Murphy at the airport in his car and that Pfeiffer and Murphy went back to the house in Palm Court, a pretty isolated development on the fringes of Henderson. It was where Pfeiffer was discovered, shot in the head. No gun was recovered at the scene.

Harvey was eager to see the scene of the crime; he wanted to get a feel of what might have happened when Pfeiffer was shot. It might tell him something. Captain Flake said sure they could go to the scene and they took off in a Helicopter from the roof of the Met police building. As they flew south, Megan sat transfixed by the sight of the glittering lights of the famous Vegas strip, downtown and paradise where most casinos were located. They turned east as they approached Henderson a very spread out part of Las Vegas.

They were set down in a paved area at the end of a short street, the houses were large, and obviously the wealthier denizens of Las Vegas preferred the luxurious isolation at the edge of the desert. Megan looked up the large house, a very large house, she corrected herself. All the lights were ablaze giving it a glittering look. A beautifully tended garden curved around the driveway.

Megan was even more impressed when she entered the house. It was a sight of luxury that she had not seen before in her life. The main door led to a large formal reception with a soaring ceiling and the room furnished lavishly, replete with richly upholstered sofas and exotic carpets. This she told herself is no home of a casino manager.

Captain Flake aware of his visitor's unspoken question, "The property records show that it belongs to Bruce Tanner, Pfeiffer's boss"

"Where is Bruce Tanner, do you know?" asked Harvey "Pfeiffer had told us that he was in Macau"

"At the moment we don't know" said Flake.

Harvey impatiently asked him, "Couldn't you trace his Cell Phone signal, if he is using a US issue phone?"

Flake was not put off by the assumption that they were slow off the block. "Yes, we do that, routinely, but it has been to be switched off since you were last here, the last call to that number was from Topkapi right about the time you left the casino and he was in Macau at that time"

Megan still in awe of the grandeur of the house and went around like a prospective buyer. The infinity pool, the vista of the city glittering far to the north all told her that someone loved luxury and had not spared any expense. This was no family home, it was not child proofed, or for that matter family proofed. The dining table for twelve was meant for visitors that needed to be impressed by the impresario, the casino mogul. Does indulgence underlie corruption or is it the other way around?

At that moment all hell broke loose in the house and outside, the cop car radios started to crackle with urgent messages and dispatch orders, Captain Flake got called to proceed to the scene of developing prime time action.

Urgently beckoning Harvey and Megan, Flake took off at a trot for the helicopter; they were soon airborne and continued to receive the update of the action at the scene. Flake shouted about the noise of the rotors that the Metropolitan Police had received a call from Dr. Murphy to a hill side resort. The fact that a man notified on an All-point Bulletin was calling emergency 911 had touched off the police action. Donna Waller was directing the action personally and was glad that Flake was nearby and could reach the hill resort faster than cruisers up the winding roads into the hills.

In any event, police cruisers were already at the scene when the helicopter landed. The incoming cars had turned their headlights directly onto the front of the small cottage perching on the edge of the slope. In the glare of the lights the detectives could see Dr. Murphy holding a gun and calmly waving them inside, the cops arriving seeing the gun had taken cover behind the cars and none had ventured to take up the invitation of the armed man.

Captain Flake fearlessly walked towards the man and held up his hand in restraint at the cops on the scene.

The tension eased somewhat and Flake continued his stroll towards the wanted professor.

Dr. Murphy was surprisingly calm and greeted the approaching officer and told him, "Everything is under control, I have the man tied securely and his gun is with me"

Flake asked him, "Who is secured?"

Dr. Murphy impatiently told him, "The murderer of course, Bruce Tanner, he shot Pfeiffer in front of me, I am the witness and then he forced me here last night and he held me hostage since then and the moment he fell asleep I took advantage of the situation, grabbed the gun and tied him with sheets". Flake extended his hand and Dr. Murphy placed the gun in it without demur. They then rushed into the cottage, inside they found a man securely tied to a chair and for good measure one leg was secured to the dining table. The man had a rag stuffed in his mouth and it was obvious that he was in distress. Flake swiftly reached across and pulled the gag. The man coughed and sputtered, his dry mouth not letting him speak. Megan reached across to the carafe of water on the table and splashed his face. A couple of policemen who had come crowding the small room untied the man.

At last able to speak, he pointed to Dr. Murphy and said, "That's him the madman shot my manager in cold blood!"

They turned to Dr. Murphy standing at the door, he appeared calm and a bit fatigued, he nodded, "That man has quite an imagination, I called the police, the car outside is his or his managers, this is his cottage and that gun I gave you is his! You can go ahead and arrest him for the murder of my friend Dr. McPherson and his own manager Mr. Pfeiffer".

The police had on their hands two murders and two alleged murderers. Flake reacted without hesitation he told them, "You two are under arrest in connection with the death of a person by gun shot, we are taking you to the headquarters"

Dr. Murphy bridled, "You want to arrest me for the murder of a man, when I have directly led to the murderer, and this is preposterous"

Flake had an answer for him, "You are not under arrest for murder, you are hereby detained in connection with the shooting death of a man here in Henderson, which we strongly believe you may be involved in, not to mention the illegal restraint and detention of a man!"

"You can't arrest the popular professor of a well-known university the students will react and go on a rampage!"

"Unlikely!" Megan intoned dryly. "What's unlikely?" asked the glaring professor turning to the voice of dissent.

Megan was unfazed, "Unlikely that you ever were popular! What did you teach—misanthropology?"

Flake put an end to this exchange by having the two suspects handcuffed and led away.

Arriving at the Met Building, they went directly to D/C Waller and described the events. Waller said they could detain the two for the night and produce the two tomorrow and be bound over for a formal preliminary.

Waller assured the detectives that the state had sufficient material for such action and in any case they had the APB to rely on for Dr. Murphy's detention.

The Deputy District Attorney Clara Dubois rushed into the conference room. Waller greeted her warmly. The Met Police loved Deputy DA Dubois, she had secured more death penalty convictions than anyone in the DA's office, not just that, twenty of those decisions had been affirmed by the Nevada Supreme Court in last year alone. A mark of prosecutorial competence was the number of convictions affirmed by the appeals court, not reversed and remanded and on that score she was a superstar.

D/C Waller was definitely glad to have her on the side of the police, and gave her a brief of the current situation. They had two men in custody right now booked and already in the holding cells down below, there has been a murder and the two were undoubtedly involved. Waller had actually started at the wrong end of the story, she explained that the San Mateo Sheriff's office in the course of investigation of a murder there, had come to Vegas and had interviewed the manager of casino and that manager was now the murder victim, the possible suspects were the Owner of the casino and the friend of the victim in California. Added to this confounding situation was that both suspects in custody claimed to be the eye witness to the murder committed by the other! A gun recovered, likely the murder weapon, was just then on fast track processing at the crime lab, any trace of the ownership might tie it to one of the men.

Deputy DA Dubois listened and grew increasingly unhappy, not a winning situation. She explained that the morning appearance in the court wasn't her worry; they could file a series of charges enough for the judge to deny bail as in a capital case. But the preliminary hearing itself may pose the bigger problem, since the two men were offering testimony against the other, one or the other's defense counsel may ask for the trial to be severed. A direct result of separate trial would be that 'conspiracy to murder' charge goes out of the window. If the trial court denies the motion to sever the trial, then the Supreme Court may reverse the conviction of the accused on the basis that they had adopted conflicting and irreconcilable defenses and that the defenses were mutually antagonistic. Either way, a no win situation was developing. They had to find some direct evidence.

Donna Waller patted the hands of the Deputy DA reassuringly, "Don't worry, let's get ready for tomorrow, I think you are thinking far too ahead of trial and appeals, focus now on the arrests, the arresting officer is Captain Flake here and in case you need corroboration then we have these officers from California" she said indicating the two.

The two were in fact very confused they were here investigating the murder back in California while the likely suspects were up against the same charge in Nevada.

Harvey the spoke up, "We need to talk to the DA's office back in Redwood to find what we need to do to arraign either of them for the murder in San Carlos"

The Deputy DA considered that for a moment and shook her head, "We have a better chance of conviction here, they were arrested with the weapon used to commit the crime, one or the other may go for plea bargain and that greatly increases the chances of a guilty plea for a second murder watch me bundle them up, Your DA will be happy when we deliverer them for the trial there."

Megan was not comforted, she said gloomily, "This means everything rests on one of them singing or else both the cases are out the window, two murders and no murderers!"

Waller once again moved to comfort, "At the moment your work is done here, you continue with the investigation into the gaming machine back there in California, but here there are people waiting to talk to both of you, in fact they are all waiting as we speak to talk to you, In fact I am under orders to cordially invite you to meet for an informal brief on the progress of your investigation"

Somewhat mollified by the 'cordial invitation' they followed Donna Waller to the meeting with the city of Las Vegas official czars.

The conference room was quite large and the assembly resembled a town hall meeting without the raised platform for a stern presiding officer. In fact the pre-eminent high ranking man himself came forward welcoming the royalty from California. The importance they attached to this meeting was apparent; the visiting detectives from California were stars in the midst of admirers.

After what seemed an interminable round of introductions, the Chairman addressed those present, "Today we face a crisis in that our primary industry, the casinos are facing a tax demand that ranks with the bizarre, a failure to deduct Withholding Tax on repeat visitors when the casinos themselves are not equipped to monitor such activity, they are not required to by any law unless they have systems in place or suspect that some winnings are escaping tax, the last I heard from the IRS is that the flurry of activity of that agency has been prompted by a new wing called Compliance Analytics Initiative of the IRS, this can kill our industry as it is we comply with the directions on Money Laundering but this we feel is using information gathered in the name of money laundering to target tax evasion, I have lodged a strong protest with the white house and our state senators are fully on our side" he then turned to the visiting royalty, "we thank these friends from California, who first pointed out the abuse of The Patriot Act to this our most vital industry"

Megan was bursting with pride it was her instinct that said the move to use information they had unearthed didn't entitle the government do demand tax retrospectively, the Treasury should have been smart about it from the start, not retrospectively which is what this Compliance Analytics was trying to do! Is there anything in the course of time that could be made to happen retrospectively?

The Chairman of the Gaming Commission then asked them, "What have you found that could have an impact on the credibility of the industry as a whole, is it possible that disclosures regarding the gaming machines being manipulated reflect on the fairness that we so strictly ensure?"

Harvey understood the gravity of the situation, the palpable concern that the 'tax man cometh' had induced in so many people dependent on the health of an industry that depended on dreams.

Harvey stepped forward addressing the assembled with the assurance of a professional, a voice of reason, an analyst of possibilities, "At the moment the finding is that it is the work of an individual who might have used it to enrich himself, we don't think he compromised the industry, he exploited the whole industry, no doubt, but he appears an honorable man who paid his taxes and not one has anything to say of any debased motive to destroy Las Vegas, he loved this place, our focus is to only to see that if it led to his murder and bring that murderer to book. We are clear about one thing this finding of manipulation, which we have yet to establish scientifically, did not compromise the industry"

There was a collective sigh of relief, everyone there depended on the health of the casinos for their welfare, and even a fraction of the number of casinos going under would severely affect the equilibrium of state finances. Let alone casino jobs loss, they would be redundant! The enforcers without anyone to enforce.

But Megan, ever the practical one, spelt it out for them, "you may have to scrap about 15 thousand machines" It certainly put a stop to the euphoria building up among the present.

Harvey moved swiftly to contain the damage, "what we mean is that some gaming machine's control panels may have to be replaced".

It's never too late at night in Las Vegas, they were invited to be the official guests of a major casino resort and Megan was in heaven.

Chapter 15

A CALL FROM THE GRAVE

Captain Flake turned up early at the hotel to pick up Harvey and Megan; they headed to the Eighth Judicial district courthouse. If anyone thought that Las Vegas comes alive only at night, they would be disabused by the bustle of the city at 9 in the morning. They went into the courtroom and saw that two lawyers were seated at the table for defense counsel. The Judge arrived briskly at the appointed hour, barely had the court settled down when one counsel stood up and launched into a spirited attack on the conduct of the police in arresting Dr. Murphy. Flake leaned across Harvey and Megan and told them that the Lawyer representing Dr. Murphy was a well-known defense lawyer from the most expensive firm in Las Vegas. It left Harvey wondering how Dr. Murphy had zeroed in on the best available legal assistance since last night. The lawyer representing Bruce Tanner was a distinguished looking patriarch who was the leading counsel for Casinos. They were a full service firm handling the myriad issues for the Casinos but were not that well known for handling criminal defense. It appeared that

Bruce Tanner had plumped for the known name than pick a specialist for the grave charge facing him.

The defense for Dr. Murphy easily tore into the information filed by the prosecution; it lacked information of the most basic kind. He said it clearly showed the arresting officer; in this case Captain Flake had himself stated that Dr. Murphy was waiting for the police to come after he had made a call to 911. The police instead of thanking a good Samaritan who had secured a murderer had instead arrested him, a man who had been abducted at gun point from the residence of the kidnapper and had been deprived of sleep through the night and day. The lawyer went on cite the fact that the person in question was a professor and not a seedy night club owner, this was an indirect denigration of the other arrestee. The prosecution tried several times to stop the tirade from the lawyer but each time the Judge waved them down. Deputy DA Clara Dubois had been prepared for only a nominal opposition to the formal detention and the date to be fixed for the preliminary hearing; she had not anticipated such a detailed attack on the need for detention in the first place.

She played her last card, the police in San Mateo County in California had issued an APB and his detention was also linked to that. The defense lawyer briefly conferred with his client and vehemently denied that his client was wanted by the police in California in connection with any matter, the APB had been issued on the basis of a wrong notion that the professor was not at his usual place of residence or work and police had failed to sufficiently make enquiries, in fact the professor had posted the fact of his travel to Las Vegas on his Facebook page and on Twitter, a fact that would have been in the know of any of his 1000 friends on the social network. A call to any one of them would have elicited that detail. The court room was stunned into silence. None were more stunned than Harvey and Megan, who would think of trailing a suspect on his Facebook postings!

The judge immediately ordered him released and merely stated that he should be available for hearings in the case relating to the prosecution on the charges contained in the information. That left Bruce Tanner as the only suspect in the killing of Pfeiffer and taking into account the murder occurred in his house and that he was apprehended by police following a 911 call by a person who claimed to be an eye witness, he was ordered held without bond, a date for a grand jury hearing was fixed. Bruce Tanner appeared visibly shaken by the turn of events, his lawyer made a feeble attempt of 'his word against mine' defense. The judge disagreed and said that it was matter for the grand jury to decide.

The court room emptied quickly, Harvey, Megan and Flake watched Dr. Murphy stride from the courthouse and hail a cab and disappear down South Las Vegas Boulevard presumably heading for Henderson Executive Airport. The dispirited trio made their way back to HQ there a post mortem of the happening in the court was under discussion. Deputy DA Dubois was certain that there was premeditation in bringing in the high priced defense counsel who was very sure, very certain of the defense that he had mounted. The only satisfaction of the morning came from the wretched state of Bruce Tanner. He will break in a day or two was the verdict.

Harvey and Megan decided to return to Redwood City that afternoon itself. Harvey had turned very pensive on the flight back. His instinct told him that it was a staged play at the courthouse. He had never seen a man as calm as Dr. Murphy had been in the court when he was likely to be arraigned as an accused in a capital case. That thing about the Facebook/twitter post also seemed a lucky break for the professor. Why would a professor rushing to Las Vegas take time to post his travel on the social networking sites? Taggart and Devlin had staked out his house and he had somehow given them the slip and made for the airport.

From the San Francisco airport they made their way straight to the office and had an intense discussion among the team. They rehashed all the things that they had done since the beginning. Harvey went up to the board and listed out the unresolved matters. Taggart said that the Ladder issue was unresolved, while they knew who removed the ladder they had not been able to figure out the caller asking the ladder be removed. The victim was shot from outside but that someone had entered the house and attempted to strangle an already dead victim. Harvey remembered one more thing; the tech guy from the Crime Lab had said that there was a feed from a casino on the victim's computer. What feed and why? What was the relationship of the professor with Pfeiffer and Bruce Tanner? Did anyone of the three Dr. Murphy, Pfeiffer or Tanner become privy to McPherson's secret?

As they sat discussing the next step, there was a call from the university; Patrick Diggs was calling about the report on the Control Board they had sent to the National Institute of Standards and Technology. Harvey and Megan rushed out and made record time to the campus. Patrick waiting for them then led down to the Information systems Centre.

Dr. Trapps looked happy, a child who has solved a puzzle, and he launched into the explanation, "The basic material is a type of resin a very specialized one and the NIST people have isolated the Carbon Nano Tube doping material as a magnetisable material that has some particular properties in varying thermal conditions. Just as you can direct a microwave beam and heat up things a magnetic flux directed at the strip would produce some heat and a strong magnetic field. That action was probably induced by means of resonance induction similar to near field wireless electric systems. To put it simply, bring along a strong magnetic resonance field close enough and the strip would heat up and it would act in an electromagnetic field. And because the resulting field would be far stronger than the field of the underlying circuit, paradoxically the flow of current reverses. Voila the control board functions differently."

He looked up to check the faces of his listeners, he sensed that the use of the word paradox meant a whole lot different to them and added, "I used the wrong word, the reversal is a well-known phenomenon in electrodynamics, what I meant was that it flows in the direction it was not intended to"

Then Patrick spoke for all of them, "You are saying that some magnetic field resonance heated up the strip and induced some electromagnetic field to alter the control board?"

"Exactly, usually the arrangement is obvious but in this case the whole thing was microscopic and needed a thermal change for induction to happen, heat—you had to build up heat in the resin for anything to happen and a strong magnetic field."

"Lighters" all three said it at once, Professor McPherson was not lighting up cigars, and he was switching on the magnetic field. The next question they directed at Dr. Trapps, "Can one have a small device in hand to generate this kind of field?"

"Sure, you can have a hand held device, but the power source would be the size of boat anchors! Unless you have new-fangled lithium ion batteries that are flexible or molded"

Megan asked him, "Can you build one of that sort? Handheld one I mean?"

"Oh Yes!" said Dr. Trapps "once you know the purpose it is easy"

Megan then told him, "Within the next 24 hours you will have the Nevada Gaming Commission as a client"

Dr. Trapps then said to them, "Dr. Patrick tells me that it is the work of one of our distinguished professors in Mathematics here at the University, I am amazed because it is only in the last decade or so that research has been happening in Nano technology and there aren't that many labs around the world that can even grow these things at high temperature. But it seems the professor not only devised some sort of circuit having a coil but also a hand held device to activate it, absolutely amazing. Pat tells me that the Doc did a lot of work for the casinos. I suppose that gave him an opening to install a circuit and bypass the regular logic and get the outcomes he wanted"

Dr. Trapps moved on to the large screen at the end of the laboratory and brought up a chart, a flow diagram, "See this is the schematic of a process, it starts there at the top and as one function is executed depending on the outcome it proceeds to the next step in the execution, It is possible that his device somehow changed the flow and proceeded to execute a command that he wanted."

Harvey noticed a laser pointer on the table nearby and picked it up and pointed at the middle of the flow chart and began to ask, "That is he starts here, and not at the top" the green laser dot moving along the chart "and the execution of the program goes in some other direction . . . . ."

"Exactly!" Dr. Trapps seemed anxious to get back the pointer from Harvey and held out his hand, "Please give that laser pointer, around here we consider that a hazardous object!"

"Why?" Harvey said quickly handing it back to Dr. Trapps, "It's just a laser pointer?"

"Yes, it is a green laser pointer and it has been tested for safety and found to be unsafe because it emits more visible light and infrared light also, both well above the maximum limit. This particular pointer", he held it up, "Emits 10 times the legal limit and so is unsafe!"

Harvey and the others weren't sure that Dr. Trapps wasn't pulling a fast one on them, "You're kidding me"

"I kid you not!" said Dr. Trapps "It's a recent discovery but there it is, check the Code of Federal Regulations and American National Standards Institute, my friends in NIST tipped me off when I called them about the Gaming Control we had sent them"

We Americans live in a dangerous world, mused Harvey, we don't need North Korea to threaten a missile launch on American soil, holding a laser pointer posed a sinister threat to our beloved academics!.

Triumphant that they had succeeded in cracking a scientific mystery and wizened at the danger lurking in everyday objects, the two detectives made their way back to HQ, on the way Harvey decided to visit the crime scene once again, calling Tilden to meet them at the San Carlos place. The crime scene would have to be re-enacted for the shot that killed, it would give them the detail of the angle of the shot.

Tilden was already waiting at the house, they went in and asked if they could work in the study of the professor and Miriam welcomed them.

In the study, Tilden pulled out the stack of Crime scene photos, they noted the angle of the head of the victim, it was thrown back and the chair which was pushed deep into the well of the massive desk had stopped the chair from toppling. Tilden started to reconstruct the scene, "We know that the Professor sat in this chair reading and the window was open . . . ." Megan interrupted him, "Reading what?" she had been absorbed in the photos. They quickly converged for a closer look and the photo showed that while the desk was littered with paper and a lot of books piled up on each other, there was none that was open or shut directly in front of the chair. What was the professor doing sitting there if not reading a book, watching the sunset? The window faced due west, but the sun would have dipped behind the hills in that direction. Working on his computer?

Harvey recalled that the forensic technician had told him that the computer had some sort of live streaming video from a casino table. They found the cable socket fixed to the table. The surveillance team had reported that a cable company had dismantled a dish antenna from the roof. They sought out Miriam and asked her, "What was the dish antenna for? And why did she have it removed?"

Miriam said that it was a Wi-Fi connection installed years ago and her husband used it in the study for talking to people on Skype or some such thing it was all very new in those days and Dennis said that it connected him to some people even in Europe, it had remained that way and since they did not need it anymore she had asked the company to remove it.

If the Professor had been on Skype at the time of his murder there was a good chance that the computer might show them the last call details. They rushed to the Crime Lab in record time and located the technician who had worked on the computer. The technician said sure there was some software installed for VoIP services. Tilden asked him in a tense voice, "Can you tell us anything about that last call on the computer?"

The technician suddenly aware that it was no ideal question replied, "Sure the computer will throw up that detail, also because of the background processing there will be looping and a small cache of the voice and image data packet will be there particularly in the older versions of VoIP protocols" and so saying he went to work on the computer and brought up the last images from that last call, after what seemed a long time, but in reality just a few minutes, the detectives and Tilden saw on the screen the visual of a gaming table.

Transferring that small clip on to a bigger system they watched several reruns of the clip. The technician then pointed to a brief flicker in the image and said the image was a screen grab of a CC TV monitor. The monitor of the CC TV system frequently refreshes the image and the flicker was caused by that.

They were now certain that the Professor was talking to someone on Skype and the person at the other end might have seen the shot that killed him. The only person who had shown any knowledge of the crime scene had been Pfeiffer, who might have seen the killer on his screen-if the call had continued, possible because they knew that the killer entered the study and squeezed the throat of the dead man, possibly it was the killer who had closed the computer. Pfeiffer being very dead the only possibility was that the system at the Casino had recorded the call. A remote possibility, but the only one present before them.

Harvey called Captain Flake in Las Vegas and told him that McPherson had called Pfeiffer just before his death and that call might have been recorded by the system at Topkapi casino. In turn Flake told him that a large scale investigation was underway at Topkapi following the disclosure of the ownership manipulation and the department had a free run of the place and the warrant covered everything. Assuring Harvey that he would ensure that the survcillance system at Topkapi was secure he summed up the situation, "So you are looking to hear what two dead people said and to see a killer at work, surely that's a call from the grave!"

Chapter 16

GAMBLING PAYS

Lieutenant Jim Boskey on hearing of Dr. Murphy's release in Las Vegas had ordered surveillance, not covert surveillance, but an overt one, there was a cruiser outside Dr. Murphy's house, and there were others in plain clothes trailing him in plain view. There were tell-tale clicks when he picked up the phone. It was a well-directed effort to unsettle the guy. Boskey wanted the cocksure professor to develop a siege mentality. Lisa Raymond from the DA's office had secured a warrant to access his financial records. The request for the warrant for search and seizure was supported by a notice from the Las Vegas Metropolitan Police that they were presently investigating various crimes and among those termed as 'person of interest' were Dr. Murphy. The notice contained a slew of likely criminal acts thought to be perpetrated by those under investigation. It gave the San Mateo DA the ammunition to file for the warrants as a measure of helping the neighboring state law enforcement.

In the morning came the news that Dr. Murphy was suing the county and the police. Megan met Lisa

Raymond in the office who seemed elated, "This is it, they have dug the hole into which they will surely fall, It is one thing to defend yourself against the mighty state, the law will rally to the helpless citizen, but quite another to challenge legitimate action by law enforcement, you'll see the law weigh in for law enforcement."

The suit as presented by a leading firm brought forward a basketful of complaints against the Sheriff's office, harassment due to unwarranted surveillance, possible unauthorized wire-tap, invasion of privacy . . . . The lawyers had gone to town on these and others. An immediate Cease and Desist order as well as a permanent injunction was sought.

The case came up before Judge Randall till recently a member of the bar now elected to the bench. He was not impressed; the city attorney said the DA's office would be presenting the counter. First up was the warrant issued by the District Court itself for a search and seizure, at the core of the complaint was the information provided by the Clark County DA on the investigation by the Las Vegas Metropolitan Police into widespread violations in Federal law and possible link to the murder there. Lisa Raymond didn't have to do much, she told the court, "The petitioner is the subject of investigation in two states, it involves two murders, an investigation into violation of Nevada Statutes of a criminal nature, and finally the violation of Federal law namely the USA Patriot Act 2001".

The mention of the patriot act was at the suggestion of Harvey, who told her instead of saying money laundering say Patriot Act that would shake his counsel more than Dr. Murphy himself.

The counsel for the petitioner rose from his seat, he had decided to salvage his dignity, never in his long career had a petition been so easily scuttled, 'we seek to withdraw the petition and my client makes himself available for any inquiry by the police" Dr. Murphy appeared furious at his counsel, tugging at his sleeve asking him not to give up, the Attorney freed himself firmly and Judge Randall ordered that the petition had been treated as withdrawn and banged the gavel in finality.

Dr. Murphy rose from his chair and turned to leave the courtroom, standing on either side of the door were Taggart and Devlin. The professor knew that this time he could not hope to hoodwink them and escape their vigil. Yet he kept up his dignified bearing and walked from the room avoiding meeting the eye of either of the police that he had taunted not so long ago. Taggart and Devlin chastened that he had earlier fooled them were determined not to fail this time and turned and followed their quarry.

They sprinted across the terminal to the boarding gate, the call had come in as Harvey and Megan emerged from the courthouse in Redwood City, Captain Flake had some momentous news, Bruce Tanner had asked for a plea bargain. The unanimous opinion among those at the court at the previous hearing had been that he would fold. The anxiety that drove them to air dash to Las Vegas wasn't just to hear Bruce Tanners' 'Mea culpa' a confession they knew was coming, but to see if the surveillance system at Topkapi had captured the live action scene of the murder of the professor in San Carlos on that Saturday.

Arriving an hour later at Las Vegas they were greeted by Flake outside the terminal and sped up into the city in his cruiser. On the way, Harvey said, "I am doubtful if anyone would knowingly record his own calls"

Flake seemed to be upbeat about the prospect of finding some evidence of the call, he said, "My hope rests on the extreme capabilities of the systems installed in all the casinos, It's the law here and the casinos vie to have the best system because If an audit ordered by the Gaming Board shows that there is inadequate surveillance that can be a big head ache for the casinos. The bigger casinos all come under a category of License termed 'Nonrestricted License' and those Casinos have mandated surveillance, so let's see If Topkapi, which is in Category B for surveillance meets that standard"

When they reached Topkapi the area was deserted, there was no yellow tape around the place but notices had been put up that the place was closed by the order of the Gaming Commission. Tour operators had scrambled to direct visitors away from the place and get them alternate accommodation. Inside a few officials from the gaming board were intent on their task, the affairs of the casino was under intense scrutiny. Captain Flake led them up two floors to the command center for Security. This had been the domain of Pfeiffer and a few of his most trusted men. The place was secure and no one was admitted without the prior permission of the head.

The command and control resembled a war room with its array of monitors and control panels. The wall on side was covered by monitors, banks of them. The banks of monitors were designated by the areas they covered, one set was the Utility, these were for the CCTV from the utility areas of the casino sometimes deep down in the bowels of the building. A second set covered the service area, meaning the staff was being monitored in every action they carried out in the kitchens, the stores, the laundry, room service, housekeeping and the myriad of services a resort had to offer its clientele. The third sets of monitors were by far the largest comprising of some 25 monitors. They were at the heart of operations for they covered the casino floor. Each monitor seemed to show the images from 8 CCTV cameras at a time. The images on the monitor screens flickered every now and then. At the console sat the security staff who kept watch on the images so that any suspicious activity could be relayed to the security on the floor. The surprise was that the whole of the staff doing the scan of the images were only 5. In fact the staff here relied more on the security on the floor to tell them what to watch, the corner of each image would blink an alert and they would focus on that image.

Captain Flake led Harvey and Megan into the corner in what was presumably the station of the Head of Security Pfeiffer, now in his place sat a technician from the Crime Lab Cyber Cell. He was switching things on and off and look up at the images on his screen which by far was the biggest one.

Rupert the technician had worked in manufacturing of surveillance cameras and recording devices, and as the manufacture of the devices had moved to Asia, he changed to a role in cybercrime cell of the Metropolitan Police.

Flake asked him, "What have you found so far?"

Rupert told him, "I am certain the images that I got from San Mateo police is from this set of monitors, see all those monitors have a provision for up to 8 or 16 displays, that's multiscreen display and some of these screens can be set for Full Screen Display. Which means that only one image from a CCTV camera is on. That's what I saw in the loop from California. I am trying to trace which of these DVR's were active for full screen display. There is one DVR here that has been pulled out and VGA cable removed, but the PC or Laptop that was plugged in was through this port that allows remote visitor, that why this DVR was set up for Port Forwarding."

"This DVR has the provision to record all the 8 CCTV channel feed that's on the screen of any one of the three monitors or record any one monitor and what I am trying to see if the missing PC or Laptop screen was being recorded".

Rupert stopped and told them in a happy voice, "We are in luck, and someone has actually recorded that call from the PC Monitor or Laptop, that call was recorded on the HDD of this machine itself. I am now going to rewind and play" so saying he pressed a few buttons on the remote and the Screen above came with the flickering image of the dead professor on his last call.

They watched fascinated, the audio did not interest them as much as it seemed that Pfeiffer was pleading with the professor for some money, but they watched the video play breathlessly. Then a sudden development, the professor looks up from the camera on his PC and moments later his head is flung back as if shot. On the screen he is seen rocking for a moment and the head comes to rest on the back of the chair, A dark hole in his head clearly visible. The play continued for a minute or so and then Dr. Murphy came on the scene and advances towards McPherson from the back as if wary that the man may turn around and challenge him. He turns to face the victim and then brings up his hands and closes it around the neck and hastily removes it, probably realizing that the man is dead. Then his hand reaches across and snaps the Laptop cover close. There it was and the viewers all started to breathe again. The three minute kill video looking staged. Yet the man had killed his best friend.

At the exact moment that Flake, Harvey and Megan watched Dr. Murphy come on the screen and was revealed as the killer, Far to the west, the Man himself gingerly stepped out of a window on to the ground at the back of the building in the university. From the shadows stepped Devlin, asking him casually, "Going somewhere Professor?" pulling out the handcuffs from his belt.

The professor stopped and looked at young Devlin a small smile seemed to play on his lips and he said, "Actually I realized that I had nowhere to go, nothing to do, the dice has rolled against me for the last time, the game is over!" and he turned and offered his hands to be cuffed.

Devlin told the professor with some satisfaction, "You are wrong professor, the dice hasn't rolled against you, you brought this upon yourself, If you had walked through the front door we would have merely followed you wherever you went, but right now you have given me the right to detain you for suspicious behavior to avoid surveillance, I have now 'probable cause' to detain you, You are under arrest and my partner here will read your rights"

Dr. Murphy told his arresting officers, "Funny you said Probable Cause, In Gaming Theory with many variables, you will many probable outcomes, the outcome here is final, practical Law meets theoretical Statistics, Let's go unless you want to linger on Campus for some more time"

———————————•◦•——————————

The Las Vegas Metropolitan police acknowledged the team from Redwood City in solving the murder of Pfeiffer and had held back from starting the formal confession of Bruce Tanner.

To Bruce Tanner the situation must have seemed hopeless; he was the sole suspect in the death of Pfeiffer. It was in his house, a gun without a trace, already under the scanner for violation of the law for the license he held under the Nevada Gaming Laws. He knew that he could not any longer hide the fact that he had stepped outside the law in transferring the shares of Topkapi to the sharks in New Jersey. The Gaming Board would not understand the compulsion that drove him to do the thing.

They reached the metropolitan police building and were in time for the deposition to be taken by Deputy DA Clara Dubois.

As they led him towards the interview room Bruce Tanner glanced at the faces around him and said to the Deputy DA, "After all these years of seeing faces at the moment of their triumph and tragedy, I clearly see from the faces that you have had some success. That puts my mind at peace. I couldn't bear the thought of being branded a murderer".

Bruce Tanner seated himself across from Clara Dubois and first time since his arrest appeared at ease. Gone was the look of gloom that had come over him when Dr. Murphy has walked free from the courthouse.

The confessional statement was preceded by the usual legal narrative and Bruce Tanners counsel agreed that it was voluntary and was not made under any duress.

Clara Dubois began by asking Tanner, "What can you tell us from your own knowledge as to the circumstances that led to the murder of Dr. McPherson in California and Mr. Pfeiffer here in Las Vegas"

Tanner was no longer the impresario, he had in the last 48 hours aged and wizened, speaking in a clear voice that rang with sincerity and earnestness.

It is not often one hears the story of the rise and fall of a man in his own words. The rise of this man was spectacular as it was unlikely. He had come into this desert town of Nevada in search of a job as an accountant. The project promoters, a group from New Jersey had seen the frenzied opening of the Atlantic City and decided that Las Vegas offered a better opportunity. They had weighed the factor of New Jersey being a difficult place to set things up against Nevada as a successful place that retained a frontier spirit.

The first misstep was the decision to build a massive tower hotel on top of the casino floor. The promoters considered the site to be ideal location as it directly overlooked the paradise area of Las Vegas which had the highest number of Casinos. They failed to read the consultant's report on the suitability of the land to erect a thirty floor tower. During construction the building started to sink due to subsidence. A flurry of law suits followed, everyone was suing everyone involved and the promoters despaired that the investment was a complete loss.

It was the occasion for Bruce to step up and take on the city and the city managers to get the plans changed and the promoters got cold feet. He raised additional funding on his own and kept the project going. By the time Topkapi got its 'Nonrestricted license' he was solely in control.

Those in the interview room and others watching and listening on the other side were fascinated; Bruce Tanner might have been recounting his tale to a biographer and not to a team from the DA's office.

The trouble began said Bruce, "When we ceased to be an attraction and couldn't get enough people in the door, the newer places were like magnets pulling visitors away from our doors. I had to keep up appearances and that's I how I created the persona of a flamboyant owner, it kept us in the news".

Bruce paused and took a sip of water from the glass in front of him and focused on his interrogator for the first time and noted that she had a kind face and then turned to the one way mirror on the wall behind which he knew others were gathered to hear this, his personal tale.

"The move of some of the bigger casinos to have a Macau branch gave me an opening, I pitched it to the investors, the same investors who had squeezed me dry all these years, but the chance to build one was too good to pass up and I got it started off, but I had not anticipated that Macau would present more of a challenge than Las Vegas to set up the casino, that place is a hell hole for an honest businessman, don't laugh that I consider myself as honest, but the truth is that I got behind on the project and to my bad luck the global crisis dried up the promised funding, the only hope that I had was to raise funding on the existing and profit making one here in Las Vegas"

"That's when I started on the road to perdition" he obviously felt the loss of self-esteem and public image that he had acquired.

Next he explained lucidly the steps that he took and the path that led him to the present situation, "For years Topkapi operated just above the line, the investors always blamed me for the extravagant displays and I confided to Dr. McPherson on the need to dress up Topkapi's financials. He showed me a way that I could divert some funds from the Macau project to do just that. Rather than leave a trail from Macau to this place, he suggested that I place the money in some international banks and have them sent to a credit union called the East Friends Credit Union, they would remit the money below the limit for cash transactions at ten thousand dollars each time and the cash would be drawn and the cash transaction never reported to the federal authority, In this way we managed to bring in about ten million."

"All was going according to plan until the credit union got busted for the unreported cash transactions, they were slapped with a fine of some two hundred thousand dollars, but Dr. McPherson got cold feet, we were never under the scanner of FinCEN but he advised that we hold back our plan for some time. He even took the entire cash back to California and put in a bank"

Clara waited for this narrative to lead to the circumstances that led to two murders.

Tanner continued his story, "Dr. Murphy was a constant shadow of Dennis, he was in the know of the arrangement between us, sometime we share confidences without realizing the consequences, I had noticed that for some time Dr. Murphy was losing heavily at the tables and Dennis was picking up the tab, Pfeiffer some-how got wind of all that cash and gently extorted Dennis, we agreed to keep him quite with small payment when Dr. McPherson decided to stop the blackmail, Pfeiffer knowing Dr. Murphy's weakness prompted him to demand money from Dennis to keep quiet"

"You may have guessed the rest of the story," Tanner hazarded "It happened that Pfeiffer called me and said Dr. Murphy was coming to Vegas and we should talk to him about getting back some of the money, I rushed back and arrived at the house and find that Dr. Murphy brandishing a gun and Pfeiffer casually pressing him about the money, Pfeiffer grossly misread the professor, once a murderer always a murderer, Dr. Murphy upped the gun and shot him right there on the sofa, I panicked and convinced Dr. Murphy to leave the place and took him to my cottage. We didn't sleep that night, I fell asleep the next morning and he tied me up and waited for nightfall to call the police, I thought my goose was cooked"

Tanner's counsel spoke up, "What are the charges remaining against my client?"

"None" Clara said in her courtroom voice, clear and clipped "You are a free man Mr. Tanner, not even fleeing the scene of crime as we hold that you were under a threat and Dr. Murphy had a gun at all times and you acted under duress"

With that she rose and extended a hand to Tanner who leapt to his feet and took her hand gratefully.

"I will have to remind you that you are our sole eye witness and after the trial in California you will have to appear in court as prosecution witness for the trial here, so keep yourself safe!"

"Oh! I am safe, safe as a baby in mother's arms, my friends back in New Jersey have, I imagine, developed extreme reticence, and they are trying to crawl back under the rock, in any case I plan to sell my house in Henderson and get back to Connecticut to cold hard winters and chop wood for the fireplace to get some workout"

As Bruce Tanner stepped out of the interview room he turned and said to no one in particular, "You know that Topkapi sank in the first place because deep down the site there was an aquifer, a geologist told me that and someone somewhere had pumped out all the water and created a sinkhole, and on that sink hole I finally built the casino. Who knew that under these desert sands there are aquifers? But it was a good ten years I don't regret it one bit!" with that the man went down the corridor happy that the sink hole that was Topkapi had not claimed him.

Once again Harvey and Megan were rushed into a meeting of the big wigs of Las Vegas, the gaming commission wanted updates on the gaming machine fidelity.

Harvey told them, "As we had told you yesterday, the manipulation of the machines were the work of one man and he did not reveal his secret to anyone, we are sure of that, we think that he got killed because of it!"

Megan added, "We don't know for sure how he activated the system to favor him, the scientists are working on it, so it is unlikely anyone else can replicate and compromise the casino machines without the special hand held device that he had created, at least not yet"

The Chairman asked him, "So you think we don't have to order recall of all compromised machines with immediate effect?"

Megan turned and pointed to Grick of the Gaming Board, "Mr. Grick will answer that, he has had a long chat with the scientists at the university."

Mr. Grick of the Gaming Board stepped forward and said "The rogue circuit works only if the coil is intact, we'll just cut the implanted coil and it won't work, all we need is a handheld laser"

Gricktronic turned to Harvey, who inclined his head in approval.

There was a sigh of relief, a recall or replacement would have cost millions of dollars. That matter settled, the chairman rose to make his announcement, "I called the White House" it was not a boast of political reach or power, it was to tell them he considered the matter warranting the highest intervention, "I have been assured that IRS is withdrawing the Notices for not Withholding Taxes based on the Compliance Analytics, we have to merely assure them of measures in our software for that in the future, so those of you here who were thinking of going to the media and raising the specter of 'Big Brother' government might have to rethink"

A full throated cheer rose from the crowd in the room.

At last, freed from the hectic activity of the day they stepped out and Flake asked them If they wanted to stay back and spend some time at the casinos, Harvey firmly shook his head pleading that they were expected to be in Court the next morning for the arraignment of Dr. Murphy, secretly he feared the lure of the table, his last play at American Roulette had fetched him a handsome 35 to 1, and Megan wanted a round at the slot machines. A fling is a fling or a jealous mistress will sink her talons into you, he told himself righteously.

On the flight back Megan had a question to Harvey, "What happens to the millions in cash you found in the Bank Locker?"

Harvey was casual, "We'll have to give it back to the heirs, and we no longer need it for our investigation"

Megan was amazed, "That's it? No money Laundering and other charges?"

Harvey was even more infuriatingly casual, "Nope, that money is clean, no one knows how that money got there, it is merely the untaxed cash of the deceased and the heirs will have to pay the tax that's all, they will have to pay something like 3 million 936 thousand give or take a few hundred"

Megan was furious, the exactitude of his answer meant that he knew something that he hadn't told her. She fixed him with her 'don't you dare' stare and Harvey quit playing smart and said "I talked to Devlin and he told me. The family is going to be richer by 6 million dollars at least".

Megan was silent for a while after that, then she turned to her partner in scorn, "Who sez gambling doesn't pay?"

In the Crime Lab, Tilden wearily switched off all the lights except for a reading lamp on his desk, that lamp had been his wife's gift brought back from a trip to Italy, she said that the design was all the rage there, Tilden couldn't think of a more mundane thing to become a fashion rage, Yes, Italians do go gaga for design. The lab was silent and he was alone, he had just finished work on all the Lighters that had been brought in from Dr. McPherson's office. The X-ray images yielded nothing all were piezo electric fired gas lighters. He drew a box of slim cigars from his desk and picked up a lighter and flicked it on and the flame flared, he hastily drew back and saw a glow just inside the opening, he put out the flame and the glow was gone. Absently he held the lighter in his hand and pressed its side, in the opening he saw the glow, this time there was no flame. He peered closely and saw a small crystal structure just inside the opening. He continued to press the side of the lighter and bent to the lamp on the desk and as he neared it the lamp seemed to brighten. He went back and forth and each time the lamp glowed as he approached. He knew then that in his hand he held the one working model of the device that Dr. McPherson had used for so long to play at the tables in Las Vegas at odds that the Casinos never imagined.